ZIPPO

T0096253

ZIPPO

A Dark Futuristic Novel

MATHIEU BLAIS & JOËL CASSÉUS

Translated by
Kathryn Gabinet-Kroo

Library and Archives Canada Cataloguing in Publication

Blais, Mathieu
[Zippo. English]
    Zippo : once upon a time in the egg : a dark futuristic novel / Mathieu Blais, Joël
Casséus ; Kathryn Gabinet-Kroo.

Translation of: Zippo.
ISBN 978-1-55096-312-0

    I. Casséus, Joël, 1979- II. Gabinet-Kroo, Kathryn, 1953- III. Title. IV. Title:
Zippo. English.
PS8603.L32845Z5613 2013   C843'.6   C2013-900139-5

Design and Composition by Mishi Uroboros
Typeset in Bembo and Krungthep fonts at the Moons of Jupiter Studios

Published by Exile Editions Ltd ~ www.ExileEditions.com
144483 Southgate Road 14 – GD, Holstein, Ontario, N0G 2A0
Printed and Bound in Canada in 2013, by Imprimerie Gauvin

We acknowledge the financial support of the Government of Canada through the
National Translation Program for Book Publishing for our translation activities. We
would also like to acknowledge the Canada Council for the Arts, the Government of
Canada through the Canada Book Fund (CBF), the Ontario Arts Council, and the
Ontario Media Development Corporation, for our overall publishing activities.

Canadian Sales: The Canadian Manda Group, 165 Dufferin Street,
Toronto ON M6K 3H6   www.mandagroup.com   416 516 0911

North American and International Distribution, and U.S. Sales:
Independent Publishers Group, 814 North Franklin Street,
Chicago IL 60610   www.ipgbook.com   toll free: 1 800 888 4741

To the dead

To those who resist

The intention was clear: to set to words the intensity of the demonstra-tions at the Summit of the Americas, held in Quebec City in April 2001. To speak of the FTAA, the Free Trade Areas of the Americas. To share our belief in something else. Then in Genoa in July 2001, a protestor was shot dead by police at the G8 Summit. September rolled around. There was fear and darkness, war and cold. Borders were shut tight as fists were clenched, and the writing was put aside. And so there were hundreds, even thousands of us, standing in opposition, saying 'no,' getting organized. At the same time, there was Tunisia, Egypt, Libya, Yemen, Syria and Palestine. There was the Black Bloc from Seattle. There was Quebec Rostock and elsewhere, the suburbs of Paris and London, the anarchists in Athens and the Occupy Movement. Then came the Quebec Spring of 2012 and the glorious red and black strike. It was and still is a situation of necessary revolt. So again we found ourselves confronted by a period, a time. An era. One of international mutiny, one that has brought us together again, in spite of ourselves, in anger. It's the speed with which freedoms were suspended and torture regained its rights, it's seeing brutality knocking at the gates of the cities and burning like a meteor ripping through our skies that finally drove us to write the story of the days before we will, perhaps, surrender. All actions, all words, all free thoughts must be expressed and welcomed. Always. At all times.

Mathieu Blais and Joël Casséus
Montreal, 2010-2012

A BILLION BLOWS OF THE
NIGHTSTICK BEFORE IMPACT

The incision was perfect and fresh despite the passage of time. Carved into old and poorly maintained asphalt, Villanueva bore it as one would an old scar. It gave the city a one-eyed symmetry. From east to west, from top to bottom, it ran through every neighbourhood, reaching all the way to the Canal. Old industrial McCarthy Boulevard was like the line that divided the hordes, even though the same afflictions could be found on either side. A succession of abandoned factories and nameless buildings lay in ruin. Shouts lacking commitment and invisible poverty. A curse.

The little one was used to it. Accustomed to the Port District with its flora and fauna, she appreciated the silence that hummed there. She loved the vacant buildings that she saw each day, hollow as the skeletons of so many ancient monsters. She respected the crazy weeds that cut a path between the concrete slabs of the viaduct. Day or night, she would rather walk in its shadow than sleep fitfully in the No. 55 bus. She walked along McCarthy to get to work. Other than the old man, she never met anyone along the way: no gumclackers, no macoutes. Not even a graffiti artist embellishing a wall.

Alone.

Just the little one and her footsteps. And the old man's flesh and bones.

She had met him for the first time near the former dollar parking lot, just down the hill. The lot had once belonged to the Italian, but now it served as a dump for entrepreneurs trying to avoid paying the landfill fees at the municipal garbage heap. All neighbourhood activities revolved around the site. Seagulls and rats trailed after the garbage trucks. Once their cargo was unloaded, the area fell back into its usual apathy and despair, swallowing up all movement like a lake swallowing a stone thrown into the water. The old man earned his living there. He was the only gumclacker working the dump. He was just eking out a living.

Coco Parking.

One Dollar.

The neon bulbs had burned out long ago but that hadn't kept the old man from installing his pallet under the old sign. He led a simple life. He wasn't troubled by the presence of others. Table scraps, objects that he found and patched up, a few dollars and some brainade: he didn't need much more than that. Maybe a dog. Maybe not. He wasn't sure. The little one's determination to insert herself into his daily routine had changed everything. He ended up tolerating her presence. She ended up believing she was irreplaceable. Over time, they had developed their habits. Now he awaited her arrival like a cat awaiting its next meal.

And she came back every morning.

Against all expectations.

"Christian charity," she said. "Love thy neighbour."

She had also managed to teach him some proper manners and in exchange for a cup of coffee, she had earned a few confidences. Week by week, month by month, the old man softened. He no longer tried to slip his hand up under her skirt, he avoided coarse language and stopped arguing with the drivers who sometimes crossed the viaduct. But most importantly, he no longer drank when she was around. Sometimes she dropped a coin or two into his tin cup, making him promise not to do anything foolish with the money and smiling indulgently at him as if she were his mother. He led her more deeply into the shade of the viaducts and showed her his most recent finds. An old transistor radio, a bicycle. A frame holding a picture of the Eiffel Tower. The little one felt hopeful: a piece of humanity's survival imprisoned in the body of an old gumclacker.

A flower crowning a pile of shit.

All along McCarthy, once a busy industrial thoroughfare, lampposts rose above the pavement like gallows. The little one liked the shadows they cast on the sidewalk. Full and round, long and quickly dissolved. She carefully stepped over each one of them, increasing her pace as she neared the old man's dwelling. When she reached the sign, she called to him. That morning there was no answer. She bent to pull back the cover that served as his door and poked her head inside. There sat the old gumclacker, propped up and motionless against the wall. A clean cut above his collarbone left a strangely empty space. A great deal of his blood covered the ground. The old man's lifeless head lay between some old condoms and an alarm clock.

The little one's heart exploded like a star.

Definitive. Irrevocable. Just as it always happens here.

NOTICE

On one of the pillars supporting the bridge that led into the city, a gumclacker had written a sentence. The letters were immense. Everyone taking the highway north to enter the city saw them.

THERE IS STILL TIME TO STOP READING

It's not too late.

IN WHICH WE MAKE THE ACQUAINTANCE OF NUOVO KAHID

Kahid opened his eyes the way others open their veins. The first thing he noticed were the stains that the humidity had left on the ceiling and then, below them, the peeling wall-paper. It was hot. He put a hand to his forehead and closed his eyes again. He wasn't ready. He had a headache and his mouth was pasty, leaving him with the bitter aftertaste of tin. He heard the sounds of looting coming from the street: shouting and shots fired and sirens. He hadn't left Villanueva. He opened his eyes again. The little wooden table, the chairs, the bookshelves, the big window near the bed. He didn't know how long he'd slept or how he'd gotten back there.

And yet he had come back.

The awakening, like falling.

Trying to choke everything back into his deepest self. Erase his memory so he could start to live again. That was survival – having the necessary reflexes. He knew it. What Kahid could not forget was the smell of the room. The rank odour of his lair: brainade, the smoke from his lungspitters and something more organic, too, something muskier. There was a thrumming in his ears. He touched his forehead again. He was sweating. His thoughts felt as distant as a meteor, a thousand billion miles from Villanueva. His thoughts burned feverishly, raving above the city.

He thought about Her.

Failed to see the need to go on.

"Not now," he said to himself. "Not right away."

He sat on the bed. Searing pain accompanied all movement. He lit a lungspitter. He had no memory of the past few days, nothing to tie him to his own story. No longer knowing where these memory losses would lead, he let himself drift. He thought about opening the window but didn't. It hadn't worked for a long time now. There were butts and empty bottles on the floor. A book by Thompson. An answering machine with its light flashing. A woman's undergarments. As many dots to connect as there were empty spaces between them. As many explanations as absences.

But nothing to relieve his headache.

He had to get up. He almost tripped over the Thompson book on his way to the bathroom, where he promptly vomited. He wiped his mouth with the back of his hand and studied himself in the mirror. He squinted at his own familiar reflection: sallow skin, dark bags under the eyes. The stub of a lungspitter still burned as it floated in his unflushed waste. He turned on the tap and only when he put his hands under the cold water did he notice the stains for the first time. Big patches of dry blood. On his fingers and palms, in the folds of the joints and somewhat darker under the fingernails. He rubbed them vigorously to no avail.

The stains would not go away. They seemed indelible. He sneezed. He was cold now.

He felt the panic rise up along the length of his gut. Kahid was shaken to the core. Standing before the window of his apartment, he examined his image more closely. A layer of frost coated the window, fraying the edges of monotonous grey clouds and those of his face. He laid a hand on the glass and left its imprint. The bloodstains were still there, clearly visible. The strange feeling of no longer remembering what day of the week it was, remembering only scars and losses. New lungspitter burns from other forgotten nights had appeared between his fingers. Only the lethargy, getting a second wind. Waking up was brutal.

The hand on the window.

Him. Trying to find himself, yesterday.

One constant took precedence: the face of A*** in his memory, the memory of Her. Even if he didn't see any reason to go on other than the obstinacy of his violence and the face of A***. Then, in quick succession, he thought of the Ming Restaurant and the Pornopro District, the soup kitchen and Mr. Tavernak's bar. All those litres of brainade. Then the alleyways, the spiralights. Gunfire. Running with the breath of someone destined to die on his neck. A★★★ grimacing. Pissing blood.

The Canal. His P38.

Kahid reconnected with his suspicion that perhaps he had exceeded certain limits once again.

He tore the sheets off his mattress and threw them to the floor, fighting the urge to vomit again. Seeking support. With his toe, he turned over the sheets he had just tossed on the ground. They, too, were stained with blood. He sat on the bare mattress for a moment and looked for a straight line he could hang onto. Everything was moving fast. He rushed over to the closet and took out all his clothes. Instinct guided him to what he was looking for: a shoebox. He opened it.

He sighed.

The box was empty.

He had to face facts.

ASTRAL APHONY

Paint dripped on a brick wall in the Convention District. Advice or a warning. The city's tearful message.

STOP LOOKING FOR SUN

As if it were obvious.

Under this graffiti, the police had found the emasculated body of the old Sudanese. A subcontractor for the Italian, he'd had his testicles sliced off with a razor and shoved into his mouth. A black leather leash looped around his neck, his face contorted. Steinman's Girls had not been gentle with him. There had been thorns in their caresses in recent days, and barbed wire lined their lips.

Everywhere you went, you could feel the community's anxiety.

HUNDREDS OF THOUSANDS OF ARRESTS BEFORE IMPACT

The big reactors at the municipal landfill defined the boundaries of the Zone. With its fine rain of cinders held in suspension and its burning trash, the Pornopro District resembled the kind of snow globe sold in souvenir shops. The heat from the landfill's fires was dry. Enough to make you forget the cold. The temperature rose as darkness fell. As did the intensity of the rioting and pillaging on both sides of the fence. As did the heat rising off any bit of flesh exposed to the frigid air, musky and perfumed and offered here for consummation.

In the Pornopro District, the heat banished any thought of snow or tenderness.

Its buildings were all clumped together like frogs' eggs. Labyrinths of hallways, basements, row houses and laneways that the residents knew well and where the macoutes no longer dared to venture. Close to the Centre, separated by McCarthy and the fence. The Pornopro District offered what was needed to those who asked for it. Pipes, crack and assault rifles. Under a thin layer of ash, all possibilities lay dormant.

There were no limits.

The fence around the neighbourhood had been erected long ago. Checkpoints had been added and macoutes were posted along the wall surrounding the municipal dump, near the reactors. Sometimes a gumclacker, still clinging to hope as if to a lifebuoy, approached the barrier. A sharp explosion always followed. Never more than one shot. One lone bullet, aimed at the head, the neck or the heart, to save on ammunition. The gumclacker's body flung backwards. Then carried off with the rubbish before being torched like all the rest. New cinders in the morning and a little more heat come nightfall. No one really let this upset them. A good habit to get into and one that was well entrenched here.

Gombo had not yet resigned herself to this.

A nervous, diligent worker.

In the shadow of the reactors, she learned to manage her expectations and control the slip-ups. She would try to make another trip outside today. Swimming toward the surface, her lungs ready to burst. She would take a gulp of air from the other side of the fence as she waited to detach herself completely from the neighbourhood. Maybe go back to Steinman's Girls, the light of the Centre and all the rest. Things changed quickly around there. Much too quickly. In just one week, the number of policemen had doubled. Checking papers no longer seemed a mere formality. The residents had a hard time explaining it.

"Let me know," Steinman said to her. "I'll come get you, if I have to."

The first time they'd met, Steinman had seemed sincere. Gombo had paid close attention to what she'd said. Clung to every word, just to get out of that neighbourhood. To separate herself from the scum of the alleyways and have some protection again. The Italian and the Witch and all the other subcontractors would help only the pornopros who yielded a profit. No guarantee at all for the others. No solidarity in the trade, only in fear. And in the fascism of fear.

As she waited in line at the checkpoint, Gombo weighed her determination. Took out her sterilization certificate and her health record. Tossed her jacket into her bag to hide the Beretta she'd slipped into it earlier. Everything seemed to be in order. Behind her, a child was crying. Someone elbowed her but she didn't turn around. Steinman's Girls never turned around. Something she'd had to learn. The line was long. A shot rang out close by. Gombo was the only one who dropped to the ground.

"Halt!"

The voice blaring from the microphone was unequivocal. She smelled the gunpowder but was used to such executions. The person trying to step out of line failed to halt. The uninterrupted discharge of a magazine emptying itself took its course. The bullets severed the body in two at waist level. Blood splashed onto those who were nearest. They lowered their heads, tightened their grip on their papers and looked away. Gombo stood up and took a look around.

There were watchtowers along the fence, with snipers in each one of them. She had never paid much attention to them.

The spiralights were switched on. A siren wailed. Apprehension surrounded her. A movement in the line. Near Gombo, two men were wearing suits and worried looks on their faces. Clients, lost with the others. Far from the pure, clean scent of their wives. They were men from the part of the city that lay further uphill and had no attachments to this neighbourhood. Suits. With no names, no faces.

"What's going on?" one of them asked a macoute.

"Temporary resettlement of the population. They're setting up a security perimeter around the Centre." The policeman's answer seemed to reassure the Suit.

Gombo did not share this complicity. It was with a fear of the unexpected that she felt a connection. Strange silences and a burbling anticipation. Still motionless, the residents around her began to glance over their shoulders. Maybe they should turn back and delay their plans to flee. A flurry of cinders danced over the neighbourhood, slowly covering heads and shoulders. They were even more immobile than before, nearly dead already. Stuck in limbo. Then everything seemed to come to a halt. There was no longer any way out.

It was already too late.

Buses.

Around her, people were whispering. Buses: a string of them appeared on the other side of the gate, which the macoutes opened. They pushed the crowd back to clear the road. Standing around, some jostling, silence, and the impasse that wormed its way deeper into Gombo's heart. The buses rolled slowly in front of the crowd. Fourteen buses, Gombo counted. Fourteen buses filled to overflowing. She even recognized some of the passengers, mostly old folk. Fourteen busloads of gumclackers.

The sirens, the spiralights, the ash and the utter lack of movement.

She had to talk to Steinman. She would know what to do.

They would never let them out of there.

Now she was sure of it.

AN IMMINENT COLLISION

The press conference had just ended. Attendance had been poor. The regulars had been there. The calculations were irrefutable. The software had clearly identified it. In the cinder-filled sky over Villanueva, thousands of miles away, in a direct line with the void: a meteor. The mass and the weight of the mass and even the date of impact – everything had been compiled and recorded and calculated and recalculated. It had all been done several times over but the results remained the same. Collision was imminent.

Like a blow from a macoute, it seemed inevitable.

This time, they couldn't be wrong.

IN WHICH WE APPRECIATE THE SUBTLETY OF VILLANUEVA'S JOURNALISM

"I might have something for you."

Hue had spoken slowly, separating each syllable as he would when speaking to a child. He always did that when talking to Kahid. He maintained a paternal relationship with all the journalists who worked for him. Everything about Hue disgusted Kahid. Especially the way he repeated himself like a schoolteacher, his habit of simplifying everything as if he were talking to a halfwit. Kahid tolerated it, if only because Hue was the boss and he, the employee. And while the pay wasn't great, it was acceptable. It covered Kahid's needs. And the least offensive of Power Corporation's tabloids usually gave him free rein.

"Go ahead, I'm listening."

Kahid had refused to sit down. Hue was sucking on the end of a huge cigar.

"Freelancing as usual?"

"As usual."

"Palestine again?" Kahid asked.

Hue shook his head.

"Venezuela? Poland? The Texas network?"

"Have you heard of the ZIPPO?"

Bored, Kahid asked, "Why me? Send Zadourof…"

For a moment, Hue stopped balancing himself on his armchair. Suspended all movement, and raised an eyebrow.

"You think Zadourof would do a better job than you?"

"Of course I do. Zadourof has covered economic news since Adam Smith was found with his invisible hand in the capital's knickers."

The editor-in-chief didn't understand the allusion at all. He seemed satisfied with Kahid's response.

"I thought about it," Hue went on, "But unfortunately, Zadourof is covering the appearance of a meteor that's supposed to crash into the Earth within the next few weeks."

Kahid regarded Hue with suspicion.

"Don't worry. There's nothing more important than what I'm sending you to cover."

Hue waited for a reaction. Kahid was content to light a lungspitter.

"The nine most powerful Suits in the world are going to meet here in the city," Hue continued. "The top Suit from Russia will be here, too, and I want you to make sure the *Villanueva Weekly* is represented."

"And what are they going to talk about?"

Hue put his cigar butt in an ashtray and smiled. He mimed a conciliatory gesture, something enveloping and phoney.

"The ZIPPO," he said, without answering Kahid's question. "There's nothing more prestigious for a journalist. Nothing. You'll have a ringside seat for all the big decisions. This event is going to make history. They'll still be talking about it a hundred years from now!"

Kahid didn't share Hue's enthusiasm. ZIPPO. The word didn't seem terribly auspicious. It brought back too many bad memories. All those acronyms roused corpses in his head. He had decided to avoid them. He preferred soft news and steered clear of controversy. The two-headed rats sometimes found in the sewers, the gumclackers that some men paid to fight each other. The pornopros that were found raped and slit open lengthwise almost every morning. Nothing good came of acronyms. Nothing concrete.

"O'Donnell told me you're spending a lot of time at Tavernak's. Something wrong?"

Hue waited for an answer. He hated discussing his journalists' personal lives, but this time it was different. He was trying to quell the rumours. To find out for sure.

"O'Donnell should mind his own business," Kahid grumbled.

"He meant no harm."

"So do you have his address?"

Hue didn't respond. He put a silly grin on his face.

OVIDIAN MACOUTES

The asphalt near the hill leading down to the Pornopro District was covered with shards of glass. He wasn't surprised. He knew that the streetlamps had been broken on purpose. Although the noise of the glass under his feet announced his presence to the other gumclackers, he could also hear those walking toward him. Despite the meteor, despite the new light shimmering in the sky, despite the emptiness and the absence and the deep holes found in the bodies. No one seemed to worry about any of it. And yet— The gumclackers had restored the night's discretion and protection.

He stopped, clenched his fists. His body tense and ready to run.

Sounds of a struggle. He took cover near the wall and concealed himself in its shadow. Further off, he caught the silence and the glint of the blade being wiped on the sleeve of an old leather jacket. The macoutes. A gang of them combing the streets aboard an old garbage truck. It took two of them to toss a pornopro into the hopper. He heard them laugh.

Only after the truck had moved did he step away from the wall, this time walking more quickly. No turning back.

They were everywhere: macoutes and their vicious blows.

Farther down the hill, past the pool of blood, he returned to the protection of the alleyways. The protection offered by his own.

But he walked directly into a fence several metres high. Like the barbed wire and the snipers' turrets, none of it had been there the night before. He was sure of it. The projectors trained their white light on him.

He heard sirens in the distance.

Coming closer. He held his breath.

HOW MANY
KRISTALLNACHTS
BEFORE IMPACT

Steinman had left a message on his answering machine and
Kahid had left immediately after hearing it. He found her at
the whorehouse on Pouy Street. It was in the Centre, near
the Pornopro District. She didn't notice him right away;
she was busy issuing orders over the phone. Kahid wanted
to help but her Girls were keeping him at a distance. He
didn't insist.

Lit a lungspitter instead.

Her hair tousled, Steinman sat with a peignoir thrown
over her shoulders. Her high heels made splinters of the
glass debris that littered the floor. She was surrounded by the
most muscular of her Girls. She swore and spit. A gleam lit
her eye. She was both threatened and threatening. She raised
her voice. Finished by spitting out her orders before hanging up. The Steinman of dreary mornings. Between the
honking of horns. Steinman engulfed in the smell of smoke
and dust, raised between the shouts. Nothing new except
for the brick that had shattered Steinman's window. Except
for the hot blast of an explosion that had torn off the entire
facade of her Pouy Street brothel.

Deathly pale and ready to bite, Steinman was on the warpath.

The anxiety was palpable.

Kahid discreetly greeted two or three of the girls with a simple nod of his head, nothing more. He hung back. Old connections bound him to Steinman, even if everything else pushed him away from this universe. He settled himself near the window as he waited for her to complete her calls. In her message, she had told him that the explosion had taken place that night, while the Girls were sleeping. The majority of the building's facade had been blown up and the big window on the ground floor had been blown to smithereens. Kahid nudged the window frame with his foot. The few pieces of glass still attached fell, and splintered on the floor, startling Steinman, who had just hung up the phone.

"This is a declaration of war," she proclaimed. "You're gonna write about this in your rag of a paper and spread the word: *Inter arma silent leges*. 'In times of war, the laws are silent,' or so they say. No one is going to push old Steinman around."

Steinman only invoked her Latin when the situation was beyond her comprehension.

Kahid remained silent, seeming foolish with his breath that reeked of brainade. He didn't really understand what was happening or what Steinman wanted. He stubbed out his lungspitter on the floor, releasing the sound of grinding glass.

"The Italian's talking about a religious crusade against us. And the Witch is talking about a curse, some kind of plague that strikes every girl in the city, no matter what."

Steinman caught her breath.

"You're not the only one?"

Steinman wrapped the peignoir around herself again and inhaled deeply before answering Kahid.

"It's the whole of Sodom and Gomorrah that's under attack, my friend. Rome is burning. It's Kristallnacht all over again."

She had a tendency to exaggerate. That was Steinman: over the top and immense and casting a shadow over everything.

They had known each other for so many years. Had 'known' each other so many times.

"No one goes to work without my permission. Do I make myself clear? Until we find out who's behind all this, you tell me or Gorilla before you go anywhere, and I mean even if it's just to go pee. For now, *res, non verba*. Let's shut up and get moving before the police get here."

The Girls, still troubled by the previous night, began to take action. Nothing could be left behind. Carpets and curtains, furniture and hidden cameras: it all had to be picked up as quickly as possible. Before Steinman could grab him by the arm and insist that he follow her, Kahid began to sweep up the shattered glass.

"I didn't bring you here for that!"

"I know."

Kahid dropped the piece of glass he was holding.

"The community has dug up the hatchet. My Girls are disappearing one after the other. There's a pogrom against us. The same goes for the Witch and the Italian. Even worse for the others. Everyone is on edge."

Kahid sighed. He saw A★★★'s face again. The Canal.

"And no one knows who's behind all this?"

"You hear rumours. Nothing specific. Up 'til now, not one body's been found. The macoutes act like none of this is actually happening. Tomorrow, you'll see – no one will say a thing about last night's explosions. Or about my Girls disappearing… We're drowning in indifference."

"I'll try to find out what they're saying in the halls of the Empire."

"I knew I could count on you. One last thing, though. About Gombo…"

Steinman didn't finish the sentence. It was pointless. Kahid didn't add anything either before wrapping his arms around her.

Once back out in the cold November air, Kahid rediscovered uncertainty and doubt. He remembered Gombo's face. It had been a long time since she'd wrapped her long legs around him, a long time since they'd shuddered in unison. The threat seemed to be real. This wasn't the first time Steinman had seen the snow fall. And she was not the type who cried wolf without at least having tried to pull its tail.

HUNGER IN THE
COMMONPLACE

He held out his hand. Others offered a cheek. He wasn't there yet. He was cold and hungry and thirsty. His body was a hollow drum, the skin stretched over the bones. He kept his eyes open. They said a lot of things, with a lot of words and double meanings. The sentences peeled away here and there, like the old posters plastered onto Villanueva's walls. He was afraid of them now. The macoutes. It was inevitable and he knew it. They all knew it.

Well before the meteor and the influenza.

They would end up killing them all.

He thought about the ones who were still too young to have earned the honour of a nickname. About all those who'd been caught. Things change. On McCarthy, the pornopros watched out for each other. It was different with the gumclackers. They still greeted each other but that was it. In the end, the new macoutes would prevail.

It was only a matter of time.

IN WHICH KAHID BEGINS HIS INVESTIGATION

Kahid heard the click of the answering machine. He stood in the phone booth, escaping the rain. He held the telephone against his shoulder. He had piled his change on top of the telephone. The sounds of the sirens and the demonstrations almost completely drowned out the recorded message.

The Centre's prostitutes had seen their brothel blown to kingdom come. The most interested party was an old lady friend. "I need you to do what you know how to do so well and dig up some information for me. Don't let me down, old buddy. I need you."

He didn't add anything else. He hung up. If anyone could get information from the police, it was O'Donnell. He worked for everyone and for no one but himself.

WHEN DOGS BURN

THE BROWN PLAGUE WILL RETURN

McCarthy Boulevard at the corner of 32nd. The Irish Quarter. Near the abandoned construction sites. It was the third notice he'd seen that morning so he paid no attention to it, at least not any more than he had to the two others. Nearby, a gumclacker extended a hand toward him. Blood stained the old man's ragged overcoat. Kahid didn't stop. He had stopped stopping. The gumclacker's silhouette faded away behind him.

On Sundays Kahid wandered around, never quite knowing what to do. It had been raining for an eternity and Villanueva was leaking all over. He adjusted his cap. How much time now? How many bottles until morning? He had slept a little, but not enough. He knew it. His body reminded him of that. And always, his amnesia. Marking off past events. He could not ignore the tension that was building around him.

He tried to light a lungspitter but the wind made it impossible. He buttoned his old parka and turned up the collar. He cleared his throat. His fingers were white with cold, the circulation almost at a standstill. He ducked into an alleyway to take refuge from the wind. It smelled of urine and garbage. Irregular breathing, too: a gumclacker's snoring. Everything around him was dying, everything caught in a tangle of knots.

He sought out moments of serenity. Of peace. He endured his temporary sobriety and used the time to repair the slivers and shards of his memory. The ZIPPO would start soon enough but he still had plenty of time. He ventured into the Irish Quarter with the vague hope of finding O'Donnell, who had never returned his call. Kahid had gone to his place. No one there.

He weighed the deep disgust he felt about his meetings with Hue. About the work he did. Fragments of images, a nebulous A★★★ whispering within him, living in him, borne by him and in spite of him. The city in which he had always lived seemed ready to reject him. Everything seemed to be getting stranger and stranger, day after day. Before the arrival of the horde and the meteor and the great green flame that would come to cleanse the earth and tear it all apart. Leaving it all behind.

He turned at the corner and entered a narrow laneway. He retraced his steps and found himself at a dead end. This was the first time in twenty years that he'd gotten lost in Villanueva. Something was going on. He turned around and finally made his way back to McCarthy Boulevard.

A crowd had gathered near Burroughs and Kahid joined it. Out of habit rather than out of interest. Passersby were pressed up against each other. Mass asphyxia and plenty of elbowing. Tension. Then an odour descended on the crowd, fetid and dirty. He observed the faces around him. He was not the only one. The farther forward he went, the more the faces changed: curiosity, perplexity, disgust. He almost regretted not having stayed at home where it was warm.

There was a fire in front of the gumclackers' shelter: a pyre. Its smoke stung eyes and irritated throats, keeping gawkers at a distance. People were jostling each other. Stepping on each other's feet. The embers' heat lifted grey ash a few metres overhead. Kahid found nothing to reassure him. He hid his nose under his scarf. There were no macoutes, only passersby who had stopped to watch. Only dozens of dead dogs that the mourning gumclackers were throwing into a stinking, revolting inferno.

People in the crowd began to murmur. They were all emerging from their torpor at the same time. The gumclackers threw their dogs' carcasses into the fire. Dead dogs by the dozens, all decimated by the Epidemic. No one understood what was happening; no one wanted to understand. No one was outraged either. No one felt anything but resignation. A superficial curiosity. Nights were becoming more and more difficult for all concerned. Winter was coming.

A gumclacker raised his voice when the last carcass was tossed into the fire.

It was a strange guttural chant. It demanded the crowd's respect. The people felt its sadness, too. Sincere, heartfelt.

The man continued until the flames died down. The crowd dispersed. Tomorrow, no one would even talk about what had just taken place, not even Kahid.

It had been a long time since anyone had taken an interest in the gumclackers.

DEPORTATION

O'Donnell wouldn't be coming back. He was sure of it now. He would leave all his crap and everyone else's crap behind. He had even thought about setting a fire before leaving. Cinders upon flames upon charred corpses of memory: burn it all to the ground to camouflage it all. Like for everything else, he hadn't had the nerve. Letting his mind review scenes from the past few days, one at a time. Twisting a rosary of superimposed, hazy images. Enough memories to forsake it all had brought O'Donnell here. With his rags. With the pitter-patter of the rain on the metal roof of the bus. With the water swallowed by the manhole cover near the sidewalk. The dampness and the cold.

He wouldn't come back here again. Never again.

Even if he were cold, even if he didn't know where else to go. Going back was no longer an option.

He knew he'd been lucky. It had already been a few days since Kahid's call. Everything had risen from the mud, a fleeting glimpse of it in the fog. Stories. Rumours. Exchanges. Gunshots. And now the bus was late. Even if he hated his own decision, he had to tear himself away from this place. He had to disappear like the rest of the people who had once been able to exist here. The Irish Quarter smelled of piss and death. Even the rats thought twice before entering the area. Nothing signalled a return to anything at all. That was the way it was now: an absence of dreams, an absence of life.

An aphony.

Riots had broken out on Burroughs Street. O'Donnell had found himself in the wrong place. The gunshot. The Canal. Before Kahid's crazy night-time call. The first call had forced him to ask overly indiscreet questions of powerful people. The rumour had spread as quickly as a slap, fast enough to make a low-class Irishman like himself try to fly under the radar for another few weeks. No one was reporting on what was happening here. Not even that dog Kahid and that piece-of-junk rag he worked for. Before all this got lost in the webs of anonymous lives, the smell of blood and shit would draw the vultures.

Kahid always followed right on their tails.

The bus that O'Donnell was waiting for would not come. He felt the certainty of it. The same certainty telling him that the entire city was falling apart and that nothing worked anymore. And he was cold. He was too old for this nonsense and no longer had the patience to endure it. He was a coward and he reeked of fear. His hands were sweaty, his body all angles. He had adopted the habit of escaping unscathed and had earned a reputation for it. He pulled his hood over his head and ran across the street. He dashed into a store and slipped between the aisles, absorbing the heat of the place as he studied the cars parked near the window. Then his eyes met those of the cashier.

They acknowledged each other with a quick nod.

"So about Morgan," O'Donnell ventured, "she doing alright?"

"Very well," said the cashier. "She said to say hello, by the way."

"That's nice to hear."

They didn't really know each other. He'd met the cashier at the Italian's. O'Donnell had dated the man's sister in another life but couldn't seem to remember his name. They had never really had any kind of connection and Morgan definitely wasn't sending him any pleasant greetings. The exchange had been polite, fitting for those who don't wish each other any harm. In this neighbourhood, everyone knew each other to a certain extent. And for some time now, O'Donnell had elicited only looks of sympathy.

Times had changed for O'Donnell, too.

He stashed two bottles of brainade in the inside pockets of his coat and approached the cash register. The cashier frowned.

"Hell of a woman, your sister," O'Donnell hissed into his ear.

He felt the cashier stiffen behind the counter. This was clearly a sensitive subject. He saw what he was looking for behind the register: those little Dutch cigars. Unaffordable and unattainable.

"Such nimble fingers," O'Donnell continued, "and an ass that…"

Before he could add another word, one of the bottles slid out of his pocket and shattered on the floor.

Once again, their eyes met. Sharp and quick.

Before the cashier had time to react, O'Donnell tossed a good dose of Cayenne pepper at his face. He leapt over the counter and snatched a few boxes of cigars. Morgan's brother rolled on the ground, shouting and desperately trying to get his hands on the sawed-off twelve-gauge stowed under the counter. O'Donnell kicked him hard in the stomach before making a dash for the old Impala he had seen outside. He'd find a way to get it started.

In his rush to escape, he'd forgotten to replace the broken bottle.

He had always hated a job poorly done.

STIGMATA

The residents of the Pornopro District all had something to escape from. For the most part, it was the neighbourhood itself and what it represented. A cage locking down under high surveillance. A double boiler coupled with intolerance. The pornopros had to produce a medical card attesting to their sterilization to get permission to leave the District, but the other inhabitants were simply no longer allowed to leave. There were those who still tried to gain access to the paths of liberty, voices raging and fists clenched.

The runaways had been shot. Justice was swift on that side of the fence.

Adding only the cost of the cartridge to the account book. Cold mechanics: no lawyer, no judge, no waiting, no delay, no report.

On the front of the Southern District's control post, there was some graffiti, which had faded from black to charcoal grey over the years. No one had bothered to remove it. An unskilled hand had sprayed it there.

RAPISTS

A different hand had added the 's' at the end of A★★★'s word. The difference in colour was proof of that. The accusation didn't seem to bother the macoutes. But then it served as a curiosity, a monument.

Only the Brown Plague from now on.

Only the warnings of an imminent end.

HEBEPHRENICS

"Nuovo Kahid. *Villanueva Weekly*."

The woman hesitated before looking in her filing cabinet.

"You work for the *Villanueva Weekly*?"

She seemed impressed. Kahid sighed.

"And…how is it?"

Two million readers and not one of them read anything other than the sports section. "Could you hurry it up, please?"

The woman complied. The sound of a loudspeaker temporarily eclipsed the brouhaha of the ZIPPO Summit.

"It's your safety that concerns us."

Kahid was almost trampled by a pack of journalists.

"That's our only motivation."

Another sound almost shattered his eardrums.

"It justifies the extraordinary measures that will be taken. Phase One has already begun."

He cursed Zadourof and his idiotic meteor. Cursed Hue and the louche rag he worked for. Cursed his whole damn absurd existence. Loathsome. This city, this crowd, this stench.

The ZIPPO.

There was a rapid inventory of the summit's various security measures. Kahid jotted down some figures: new contingents of soldiers just outside the city and around the hotter neighbourhoods, new water cannons, significant numbers of Taser guns. The erection of a protective wall around the Business District where the Summit would be held.

"We believe in strength, unity and order."

Kahid laughed and thought of Mussolini.

The phrase was drawn straight from an immutable fascism.

The journalists jostled each other when it came time for the question period. Already having what he wanted – names and numbers – Kahid withdrew. The newspapers would all relay the same information and cite the same sources and address the same aspects of the question. Journalism was nothing more than a shadow of what it had once been. It had become a mere conduit for the various powers at play.

There were now empty places near the buffet and Kahid took the opportunity to slip into one.

"You're not going to listen to the end of the conference?"

The young woman behind the buffet who had just spoken to Kahid was looking for company.

"And you? The ZIPPO makes you want to learn more about it?"

He smiled at her.

"Yes, a bit. I find the question fascinating." She batted her eyelashes several times. "You see," she said, changing her tone and moving closer to Kahid, "I think They have plenty to hide…"

Her eyelashes fluttered a few more times before she completed her thought. "They're not telling us everything."

Silence.

"Is that what you think?"

He had meant his last sentence to be sarcastic, detached. He didn't want to talk. He didn't even want to be there. He was tired of dealing with paranoiacs and the system's other mental cases. He loathed them. His air of false interest was insufficient. She was even more ignorant than she had first appeared to be.

"I'm sure of it," she said.

She leaned further over the table separating them.

"Like the Madagascan grocery on the corner. That was Them, too."

Kahid raised an eyebrow and she took the opportunity to bat her eyelashes several more times.

"They blew it up to level the playing field with the Texas network. They're everywhere…"

She stopped. There was a silence before she started up again, almost shouting now.

"Yes, it *is* true…you should write about Them!"

"Who are you talking about?"

"Them."

"Them?"

She moved toward Kahid. Her breath stank of alcohol and tobacco. Her fluttering eyelashes, tapping out a rhythm, ultimately began to worry Kahid.

"The ones bringing the ZIPPO with them. The ones the Authorities protect while the rest of us starve to death. Those guys, over there." She pointed to two Suits standing near the back and conversing in low voices. "Her, too," she said, now indicating an elegantly dressed woman who had just come out of the ladies' room. "Him!" she cried. "Him!"

This time, she was almost screaming as she directed Kahid's attention to a journalist questioning the Summit's spokesman.

"They're here! They're everywhere!"

The young woman became hysterical and Kahid backed away from her. The buffet table tipped over. Someone shouted and an alarm went off. Inside, in his head. A waiter tried to control the girl but it was a lost cause. She had colossal strength. People were beginning to stare. Indignation travelled from one mouth to another. Two men in suits quickly picked up the young woman and hauled her to the back of the room.

Kahid wanted to follow her but a hand on his shoulder held him back.

"No, let it go. It was bound to happen."

Zadourof's presence was a surprise. He must have seen it in Kahid's eyes and immediately began to answer his unspoken questions.

"I was just passing by, simple as that."

"And the meteor?"

He didn't answer. Over Kahid's shoulder, he was watching a scene that only he seemed to notice. Zadourof continued calmly.

"A total nut-job and worst yet, she's not the only one. Last time, two gumclackers came in here, stark naked and armed with a couple of old Kalashnikovs. They managed to fire a few rounds before the agents shot 'em. The Defence Suit didn't even stop talking. She's one hell of a broad… makes you think everyone is going crazy here."

THE CADAVERS
ACCUMULATE

Several hours had passed. She had awakened in the back seat of a car, alone. She was cold. Someone had undressed her. Between her legs, she felt the semen seeping out. Raped. She didn't remember anything else. Nausea. Pain in her jaw. It was very dark. She knew she was probably going to die.

She moved her hands. She could scarcely feel them. She panicked, fought the urge to move her arms. Her hands were bound. The Italian had told her not to trust men who kept rope in their cars. Too many clients who wanted to play with it. She needed money. She hadn't listened.

The garage door opened. A white light swept through the car's interior, blinding her for a moment. She squinted and looked in the rear-view mirror. She watched as a garbage truck slowly pulled up behind the car. It smelled of carrion. The driver climbed out of the cab. She recognized him immediately. She frantically moved her arms despite the pain.

It was too late now.

IN WHICH O'DONNELL TAKES THE PLUNGE

The lock on the old Impala hadn't put up any resistance. He had slipped inside and played with the wires under the dashboard. He heard the click he was waiting for and the light went on. The motor turned over nicely. He leaned over to open the glove compartment and found a cell phone inside. Checked the rear-view mirror. It was now or never. The macoutes could not be far behind. He stepped on the gas. The P38 slid across the floorboard. O'Donnell uncapped the bottle of brainade he had just stolen and held it between his thighs. He lit a cigar.

He felt the adrenaline slowly leaving his veins.

McCarthy Boulevard stretched out before him. He had reached the point of no return. O'Donnell would never come back here. Not anymore. The cell phone was working so he dialled Kahid's number. He heard it ring several times. Yanked the steering wheel to avoid a garbage can burning by the side of the road. The car reacted slowly. He swore. Kahid would not answer; he never did.

Again, he spoke to a machine.

"I haven't forgotten…neither has she. It's all clear in my mind…I have something of yours. I need it more than you might think. You have no idea. I have it with me. After what happened by the Canal, I'd be surprised if it still works… If you want to find me, you'll have to dig…I'm going under." He tossed the phone out the window.

With his free hand he searched for the P38, which had slid under the seat. He didn't see the thin sheet of black ice that sent the car flying. The old Impala somersaulted through the air before hitting the ground. The sound of tearing, crumpling metal. The car slid across the cold, wet pavement for several metres before finally coming to a stop against a lamppost.

The chafing of a tire, losing speed as it rubbed against the crushed fender.

The last hiccups of the horn.

The relative silence of the accident.

O'Donnell was alright. He smelled gas and brainade. There was blood on his face. He extricated himself from the car with some difficulty. Remembered to look for it and found it on the back seat: chrome-handled and heavy in his hand. Its weight was familiar now. The P38 comforted him.

Standing on McCarthy, he was struck by the neighbourhood's pervasive emptiness. Everything was in shadows and half-tones and whispers of light. A jolt of pain ran up his left arm. He vomited. It felt as if something was lodged in his ear. He couldn't open one of his eyes. All that blood on his face. He was alive. The macoutes hadn't caught him yet. He would not go to the hospital.

That was not an option.

O'Donnell was like a rat, eternally struggling for survival.

Located next to the interchanges near the Villanueva docks, the Port District lay gutted like a fish stranded on shore. Stinking like the body of a dead dog. It was a place abandoned even by graffiti. Nothing there but the incessant circulation of cars on the elevated six-lane highway. Nothing but the sirens and the firing of guns in the distance. McCarthy had strange offshoots. The principle of division and connection. O'Donnell didn't recognize a thing. Only fatigue and the pain.

He had to find a place to stay.

GUMCLACKERS
ON THE LOOSE

"Wake up! Now!"

"Huh?"

"I think I saw a gumclacker coming up the alley…"

"And that reminds you of something?"

"I don't know. Maybe…"

"Wake me up if you remember what…"

IN WHICH ONLY KAHID
TALKS ON THE TELEPHONE

Mr. Tavernak was as interesting as an empty bottle in an alcoholic's refrigerator. He had been polishing the counter in his bar since the world began. He was the salt of the earth. He bore the same name as his father and his father before him. Mr. Tavernak knew every face and all the rumours. Observed the alliances and their mutations. Served glasses of brainade from dusk until dawn. Always lent an ear, impassively nodding his head and refilling a glass. Everyone respected him.

For all. For nothing. For the memory.

For the sawed-off twelve-gauge shotgun he kept under the bar.

He didn't have to say no twice when he refused Kahid one last drink. Kahid had already had too much. He knew it. It was still early. Too early. It had been a hard week. He didn't want to go home where no one was waiting for him. He listened to the conversations and the banalities streaming from the television that had been left on. Perhaps later Mr. Tavernak would give him another drink. His head was spinning and he felt his own life slipping through his fingers.

On the counter, a rotary phone rang.

Mr. Tavernak kept his eyes on the television but his hand found the receiver. He barked something into the mouthpiece. His eyes slid over Kahid and he handed him the receiver. But Kahid hadn't told anyone where he would be.

On the other end of the line, he could barely hear a woman breathing. "A★★★?" Kahid ventured. "A★★★, is that you?"

He was surprised by his own enthusiasm. Maybe he hadn't forgotten everything after all. His hands began to tremble and beads of sweat formed on his forehead.

An uncomfortable silence settled between himself and the woman on the phone.

"Are you still there?" she asked.

He thought he heard the sound of a waterfall during the pauses. Or maybe a river. Flowing, rushing water. It was a bad connection, the voice almost unrecognizable. Thousands of kilometres away from him, she stirred, in a dream. Far away, so very far away. He closed his eyes and tried to take stock of the emptiness. Tried either to forget or to do everything he could to remember; he didn't know any more.

His entire body had stiffened.

"Yes," he answered, "I'm here."

"You hurt me..." she breathed.

Again the silence fell between them.

"Can I see you?"

"I don't know."

Her voice was hoarse.

"I'm glad you called me. I was worried…"

She hung up. He dropped the receiver on the bar. He began to scratch at himself and he was breathing hard. He missed A★★★. Every one of their recent meetings had ended in an argument.

They wound up talking about the past, about death. About their comrades.

The same images returned. Were they at the soup kitchen or at her place? They'd had a lot to drink. The streets were wet, the air dense and humid. They were already on the run. Then everything shifted into high gear: the alleys, the running, the spiralights behind them. Someone had fired a gun. A★★★'s face, grimacing. Then the canals of the old city. His mind couldn't put all the pieces back together again. Perhaps he hadn't killed her after all. Maybe hadn't even hit her.

He told himself he'd take a shower tonight. The stains were gone but his hands were still dirty. The storm now raged inside his head. A★★★ could not be back. It was impossible. There had been a lot of blood, such a lot of blood. The voice could not have belonged to her. He had the vague memory of a telephone conversation. Before everything got lost in the timelessness of madness. A call. Someone talking to him about the Canal. The banks of the Canal.

Mr. Tavernak slid a glass of brainade in front of Kahid.

"One for the road."

But the wink Mr. Tavernak gave him was not enough to calm his nerves.

THE HIEROGLYPHIC
HORROR

WE'RE THIRSTY

New graffiti on an alley wall.

Something had been torn from the social fabric. An ability to distinguish the banal from the horrific. A vast scab, picked at with the tip of a fingernail. In the new light of the meteor. Something going in only one direction. Something that would never come back. An amputation.

And now the thirst.

Before the cold and the emptiness and the impact.

Before the final reset.

HUNDREDS OF BODIES
TO BURN BEFORE IMPACT

No one came to the Gates of Paradise anymore. No visitors, no delivery men, no one at all. Autarchy, smelling of urine and feces. The sound of flies. The cold and the moaning. The humming of neon lights. The unused wing of a hospital.

All driven back inside.

The bodies were piling up in the infirmary. With only a simple curtain to separate the corpses and the residents, they breathed the same sour air. Shared the same idea of the end. Maria had been there since the morning, pus draining from her right eye. She kept her eyelids open. Had for a long time. Luis flicked open a lighter. Put the flame near her open eye and waved away the flies buzzing around her head. The pupil did not react. Catatonia. As if her life was suddenly leaving her, one section at a time. Abandoning certain reflexes and leaving the body useless and broken. No one knew what to do. Her chest rose and fell and the faint groan escaping her lips gave proof that life was still clinging to some part of her. An ailing bird kept alive by a single breath.

Maria was thin and sickly. One step away from the grave.

At the Gates of Paradise, the idea of death was part of the daily routine.

Luis had opened a window, trying his best to get rid of the wretched odour. But the cold and the snow forced him to close it. The smell would never leave the residence. They would die here with this smell in their mouths. He was sure of it. They all were.

"She's still breathing."

Luis said nothing.

He stayed there, thinking. Her wheelchair supported his inert mass. Forgotten in the silent infirmary. He grimaced. He detested Maervick's passion for stating the obvious. Luis was more laconic. Men speak only when necessary, his father had always said. Maervick talked constantly. Tirelessly. Luis lifted his cap and mopped his forehead. Maervick hopped from one foot to the other. He chased away the flies gathering again on Maria's face.

"They'll come. It shouldn't be long now."

Luis didn't respond. His father wouldn't have either. He would have stared at some spot in the room and withdrawn back into himself. Luis did the same. He knew they wouldn't come back ever again. Maervick knew it. All the residents knew it. The doctors had been the first to leave the Gates of Paradise. Then the nurses' smiles slowly disappeared and there were more and more absences. A few weeks later, they had been left to themselves. No explanation. After that, everything quickly crumbled, disintegrated.

The water, heat and medications disappeared, making way for hunger and pain. Death was in the silence. In the indifference.

And especially in the waiting.

They consulted, got organized and stacked the first of the bodies in the cold rooms of the infirmary. Death was necessary, then expected. The Gates of Paradise: the antechamber for old, decrepit men and women who needed only the slightest push. Then one day, they came. Dressed in grey uniforms and driving a garbage truck. They did not answer questions. Shoved the residents around. They went over to the dead bodies, tossed them onto stretchers and loaded them into the truck. Thus the infirmary was emptied of twenty-seven cadavers. Departing in the dark of night.

They did not understand.

The two ancients heard the sound of an engine outside. Maervick looked impatiently at Luis.

"So, what is that?"

Luis ignored him. He squinted to demonstrate his irritation and raised an eyebrow. "It's a truck," he said. "A garbage truck."

The truck drew closer. It had to be at the entrance of the residence already. Luis glanced at Maervick, who was taking a Beretta from his jacket's inside pocket. He used his fingernails to scratch at the frost coating the window so that he could look outside.

"It's a garbage truck, all right."

The doors slammed shut and the sound echoed inside. The front door banged open and a gust of air rose up from the ground floor. They looked at each other for a moment. They heard hurried footsteps climbing the stairs and the noise of doors closing. Someone was shouting orders.

"Do you think it's them?"

Luis was convinced of it but said nothing. It was pointless.

A man kicked the door open and burst into the room. He looked at Maervick's gun with amusement. He had a submachine gun strapped over his shoulder.

"Where's Nurse Chatterton?" asked Luis curtly.

The man smiled. A second individual entered the room, a woman this time.

"Don't waste time talking to them! There's work to do."

Two more individuals, anonymous in their uniforms, made their entrance. They carried off the bodies of Charles Luogo, Roberta Barry and Old Mrs. Wickerton. They punched out the infirmary windows with the butts of their guns. The cadavers were heaved out through the openings. The bodies hit the ground with the sound of bones breaking. The blood seeped into the black snow. Icy mud was glazed the colour of rust.

One of the uniforms approached Maria. A hand rose. Maervick intervened. A siren sounded in the distance.

The noise of a heavy engine sighing and then there was silence. The barrel of an assault rifle was placed directly under Maervick's chin. Sighs. Laughter. He stepped back.

No one said a word when they grabbed Maria's body.

Her body broke on the ground like a porcelain doll. The delicate sound demanded a definitive silence. The individuals left the infirmary without a word. Maervick and Luis were alone. The infirmary had been emptied. They had nothing to say, but after a moment, Maervick spoke.

"I'm going to take them all down!"

He waved his Beretta in the air.

"So why didn't you shoot?"

Luis took the gun out of his hands and opened the barrel before tossing the empty gun on the ground.

"Maybe there's a way." Luis was thinking out loud.

Maervick said nothing. Luis looked at him.

"Big Bertha."

KHAKI-CLAD MERCENARY

He had followed her trail. Her friends had talked, her brother too. He still had the sore joints to prove it. Traces of her were getting easier to find. Black evidence on a white background. Beginner's mistakes that didn't seem like her. He was almost disappointed. Two weeks of tracking had changed his way of seeing things. He appreciated the way she had of disappearing only to surface farther away: clandestine and ever watchful. But she knew he was closing in. Day after day, hour by hour. His breath would precede the blade, so she no longer hid. She began to run. To gain time, only time. That too, she knew.

The hunt above all else.

Survival, like a second skin.

He had become the best. No one had his talent for tracking down disobedient pornopros. He hunted high heels and wigs. Not one of them escaped. He always caught them and today it would be someone else's turn.

The building was anonymous enough. The youths sitting on the steps stood and parted to let him pass. They called him 'Mister.' He didn't glance at them; he met no one's eyes. He saw that a garbage truck was parked nearby. When he pushed open the door to the building, he knew that she was there. It was inevitable. A powerful intuition.

It was here that she would die.

The Italian would be pleased. He didn't like it when one of his girls ran away. The punishment was always the same, whether it was administered by the Italian or by his hunter. He sank into the depths of the building, into its density and its silence. Stopped in front of a door and checked the number he had written on a scrap of paper. They matched. He pulled out his Luger and cocked it. Then he kicked down the door.

The whole thing gave way, cracked and caved into the opening as if torn from its musculature.

He had stopped counting the number of times he had done this.

The odour of dust preceded that of the blood. The flesh was bruised and warm and still sticky. He had entered the apartment expecting to find the girl there. He found her dead, her body riddled with bullets. They had beaten him to it. He stepped forward and came face to face with a man dressed in khaki. His reflexes were lacking. But the hail of bullets from the TEC-9 that tore off his face more than sufficed.

The hunter was dead before he hit the floor.

IN WHICH WE LEARN A BIT MORE ABOUT THE ZIPPO

I ♥ the ZIPPO.

The inscription on the T-shirt the saleslady showed him was covered in colourful sparkles. Kahid pasted a silly smile on his face. Big and bombastic, the ugly fat woman he was questioning stared at him intently. He stepped back to get a better view of the whole and spilled part of his drink on his shoes. He had no idea how many drinks he'd already had.

"What does the ZIPPO mean to you?"

Kahid had a hard time hiding his boredom.

"It's a great merging of all peoples..."

She held her breath before continuing, almost embarrassed by what she was about to say.

"It's practically communism."

Kahid turned off his tape recorder and downed the brainade in a single gulp.

"Superb," he said. "Absolutely superb."

There was music, clowns, acrobats and dancers. The celebration at the convention centre was like a ticking time bomb, ready to explode. Immense and luminous. Pretzels shaped to spell the word ZIPPO were for sale in the cafeteria. Nothing had been left to chance. They were announcing the arrival of the first emissaries.

"You're sure you don't want to buy one of my souvenirs?"

The kiosk saleslady's voice evaporated behind him. The noise of all the commotion spread. Kahid crept over to the bar. His press card gave him access to the open bar and he was planning to make up for lost time. The general stupidity of the place frightened him. Despite the anaesthetic effect of the brainade. Despite his guts forming a ball as tight as a nest of snakes. Despite the thirst he could no longer control. All the balloons and the music and the souvenirs and the Suits and the macoutes: all if it scared him to death.

He had no trouble finding a vacant stool. The waiter barked something at Kahid so he waved his press card in his face.

"A real circus, eh? It's absolutely fascinating…"

The voice was familiar. He turned around and found himself nose to nose with Zadourof. He weakly pushed him away. Zadourof was holding a brainade that had been served to him in a wineglass. He reeked of alcohol as much as Kahid did.

"I don't even know what I'm doing here," he said, shrugging his shoulders to excuse himself.

Kahid inspected the bottom of his glass, which was already empty.

"You're not alone there."

Zadourof looked grim. He frowned and bent toward Kahid, signalling him to come closer. Despite his natural distrust, Kahid did as he was asked. He had never liked Zadourof.

"I have a secret to tell you," he whispered.

Kahid leaned away for a moment to stare at his colleague.

"Someone's tailing you."

This time Kahid frowned and grew serious. Zadourof slapped the counter and laughed like a fool. He was even drunker than Kahid. Felt the free fall that had begun long ago. Kahid got up to leave the bar. Disgust engulfed him like a contagious nausea. His body was attached to nothing and stripped of everything. Unable to distinguish true from false. Unable to figure out if Zadourof was telling the truth.

"But it's nothing to worry about, Nuovo!" Zadourof continued. "The big meteor is going to blow us all to bits!"

He was shouting now but no one seemed concerned.

"We know damn well how this is going to end!"

Kahid did not turn back. Let himself be carried away by the crowd. Clinging to the balloons and decorations, Zadourof's laughter followed him at a distance before completely dissolving into the uproar.

Then all of a sudden things seemed to accelerate around him. People were running on his right, elbowing each other on his left, and the Summit's central corridor rapidly emptied.

He grabbed one of the conference organizers by the arm.

"Where's the press conference?"

"I don't know!"

The panic etched on the organizer's face reached deep into Kahid's gut.

"There's a bomb in the lobby. The police are going to blow the place up in a few minutes!"

LIKE A RAT

Near an old folks' home. In the same emptiness. He didn't remember how but he had managed to convince the old landlord to let him take the room. The rain had washed away only some of the blood on his face. He had an ugly mug and he knew it. And yet. He had found himself there in a filthy, poorly-lit room with a window opening onto Villanueva's abandoned ports. He had not given his name or any other information and had paid two weeks in advance. Going underground was O'Donnell's only salvation now.

He would have time to lick his wounds. Take stock of the situation. Steal food and a purse or two. Nurse himself back to health. As long as he could hang onto his hideout. As long as no one was on his tail. As long as the macoutes didn't come knocking at his door.

He would stay there a few more weeks. Maybe in time the macoutes would calm down. Maybe they'd find someone else to hunt and turn their attention elsewhere. The end of the ZIPPO summit would surely improve the situation. Calm things down.

He took the P38 in his hands before entering the residence. He stayed alert, tried to spot the clues. Reasons to flee, reasons to pull the trigger. Reasons to kill.

"If this is going to go badly…"

He didn't finish the sentence. He had never killed anyone. The mere thought of it turned his stomach. He wasn't sure that he would pull the trigger when the time came. Despite the macoutes and the meteor. Despite the fact that Villanueva was sinking ever deeper into the doldrums. He preferred the shadows, sneak attacks. A job well done and full of nuance. Refined. Subtle.

The robbery.

The knives.

He had seen and heard many things in his life but he had never seen the city in such a state. He was probably going to die. He could feel it. Considering what they were saying about the pornopros and the gumclackers and all the other lower-class members of his species, it was only a matter of time. Nothing more.

He tightened his grip on the P38. The weapon had a hold on him. It was the direct link to how it all began. It had belonged to the ones who ended up on the banks of the Canal. An extension of Kahid's arm.

Vengeance.

There was nothing in the room. An emptier emptiness. A void in the very heart of an even greater void. The dust, the smell. Someone else had already hidden there. Stained clothes lay in a corner, on the floor. A window was slightly ajar; the hum of the highway could be heard like the sound of waves on the shore. And already the muffling of noise that always accompanies the first snow. Black and damp. Cold. He closed the window.

A stab of pain shot up his left arm.

He needed a drink. The thirst, terrible and profound.

In the end, the pornopros had failed to trust him. His reputation as a thief and a shit-disturber stuck to him like a second skin. No one trusted him now. All those who played the same game had ended up murdered in commissary cells. A purge. There were too many blades glistening in O'Donnell's back for him to try anything.

Even Mr. Tavernak had cut off his credit.

A rat, swatted away with a broom.

Outside, he could see nothing clearly. Tones of grey and black swept about by a cold wind. The window reflected his face. The swirling black snow rattled against the glass. He had lost weight and his hair had gone white. He had grown old almost overnight. He felt nothing inside, as if all his organs had been removed, leaving an empty shell.

In a moment of brightness, O'Donnell saw the meteor shining in the night sky.

He thought of A*** but didn't understand why. Again he saw white flashes streak across the sky, illuminating the bodies near the Canal. Then a glimpse of their faces. An instinct for death drifted over Villanueva. From now on, the rancid smell from the factories in the lower town would merge with another smell, the smell of death. A fetid odour of dead flesh and putrefied meat.

He closed the curtain and stretched out on a filthy mattress.

He thought of all the pornopros who had surely washed up onto the mattress in this room. You couldn't take pleasure here. It was impossible. The result of the emptiness, the all-consuming void. When legs grip like a vise and the cries of faked orgasm resound. The rotting mattress. Offering oblivion for a fistful of money. Villanueva was foundering.

The sound of a motor interrupted his reverie.

Another garbage truck, for sure. There were more and more of them.

Once again, the night would be long and sleepless.

HESITATION

The afternoon of an endless day. As long as a line to wait in.

"Two pints, papi."

A bill appeared on the bar and made its way to Mr. Tavernak's hand. Mr. Tavernak placed two pints of brainade on coasters. Staccato noises and the thrum of traffic outside. A man of few words, he stayed there. Leaned his back against the bar, keeping his distance. The two men were not from the neighbourhood and brought with them the smell of carrion. Mr. Tavernak could recognize trouble when he saw it, and this time he knew whom he was dealing with even before the smaller of the two put his Luger on the bar.

Mr. Tavernak lit a lungspitter.

The atmosphere was still relaxed and amiable. Mr. Tavernak had seen the gun. If blood was going to be spilled, it would be by mutual agreement.

"Where's Steinman?"

The old bartender remained silent.

"Steinman. Big redhead, about fifty years old? Queen of the neighbourhood whores? Where is she?"

The bartender's silence, strengthened by the force of habit.

The uglier of the two slapped the bar with the palm of his hand. Mr. Tavernak didn't bat an eye and moved slowly. He stubbed out his lungspitter in a nearby ashtray and approached the two men.

"Can I get you anything else?"

His voice had been polite. Calm and even.

The smile and the glances they quickly exchanged were enough. They would get nothing more. They stood slowly and the smaller one discreetly put the Luger back in his pocket. Using his thumb and his index finger, the uglier one mimed shooting Mr. Tavernak.

"Next time," he said to himself. Next time, he'd shoot before he'd open his mouth.

IN WHICH WE MAKE THE ITALIAN'S ACQUAINTANCE

The telephone rang in the next room. Ceezure paid no attention. He scarcely heard it. He was absorbed in what he was seeing. The immaculate white of his shoes clashed with the ink-black blood seeping across the floor. Before the blood, there had been the sound of someone unfolding plastic, the hum of the traffic outside. A shout.

Now the blood was spreading dangerously close to his shoes. He would wait a little longer, until the last minute. The telephone was still ringing next door. It had been ringing for quite a while. From the moment the pornopro had hit the floor. The blood gently touched one of his shoelaces.

"Bitch," he thought.

In his hand, he held a pornopro's advertisement, a page he had torn from the *Villanueva Weekly*. It announced the ten thousand positions that Plasticine Girl offered. He whispered her name with a nostalgic sigh. She had earned her fair share of money and glory for them – for him and for the Organization.

Only to end up as a pile of dead flesh bleeding out on his office floor.

What a waste.

She had tried to escape but by running, she had broken ties with her sole protector. He didn't understand what was happening. She was the third girl this week to leave him. He had tried everything. The carrot and the stick. Cash and coca wine. Nothing. Unmanageable pornopros: they didn't deal well with the changes weighing heavily on Villanueva. The increased number of macoutes in the neighbourhood had increased the number of rapes. The night could not offer the same kind of privacy it once had, now that this damn meteor was pissing light all over the sky.

It wasn't over and he knew it. Several more would give it a try. A girl's duplicity was inevitable. They would all end up betraying him. As soon as they had the chance, as soon as they thought they could earn more elsewhere, they'd all end up doing it. He had simply learned to limit the opportunities. But now everything was changing and this thought depressed him. He would need a dozen hunters to keep the pornopros working for him under control. Even when they didn't get a stiletto stuck in their eye, good hunters were hard to find.

The blood had now reached his white shoes.

"Hell of a time to live in," he thought. "Hell of a century."

A young woman burst into his office. He raised an eyebrow. She tried hard to ignore the body lying gutted on the floor. Ceezure stared insistently at her. Impatient. His two feet soaking in the pool of coagulating black blood.

His tolerance for the people he worked with was rapidly diminishing.

"They want the Italian on the phone."

He growled something and the woman immediately disappeared.

The Italian. He hated being called the Italian: he preferred Ceezure and always had. He ran his hands over his face, holding them over his eyes for a moment. Tasting his fatigue. It was probably Steinman or the Witch asking for him. They were the only ones brave enough to still call him the Italian. And then, he just didn't give a damn. Nothing could surprise him. He didn't expect much out of life anymore.

He entered the room next door. The young woman was holding the phone and he grabbed it out of her hand. Steinman's voice greeted him like a cold shower.

"Where is she?" She was almost shouting.

"What do you want?"

He didn't want to talk to her. He thought of the porno-pro growing cold in the next room.

"Plasticine Girl," she spat. "Where is she?"

With a wave of his hand, Ceezure signalled his secretary to go away. He sat down in his chair, held the receiver between his neck and chin. Opened a desk drawer. The conversation was suddenly getting interesting. He couldn't see the laser beam roaming across his forehead.

"Who?"

He took a flask of brainade from his pocket and smiled.

"I know very well how you treat the girls who want to leave you, so where is she?"

"Plasticine Girl is gone? That's impossible! I'm sure I'll adjust, but..."

He didn't have a chance to finish. A shot was fired. The window in front of him shattered. He threw himself to the floor. The bullet had just missed him. It had pierced the chair's leather, leaving a large hole. He remained silent for a moment. Incredulous. His eyebrow raised, his mouth still agape. With a trembling hand, he searched for the assault rifle he kept under the desk.

Steinman heard the sound of gunfire.

The call was cut off.

BLOCKAGE

It was cold and hearts of stone were melting all over the city. Winter was fraying at the edges of Villanueva's harsh angles and the trees, like scarecrows. Black ice, black snow and a howling wind. It was enough to make you go crazy if you weren't already.

"It's probably the Canal."

He didn't answer. It seemed unlikely. The Canal generally breached its banks in the spring, not at the beginning of winter. Two former municipal employees mechanically pulled up the sewer covers. They were unemployed now. For several weeks, Villanueva had no longer been able to pay salaries of that kind, not with its money tied up in the ZIPPO Summit. They volunteered to maintain the infrastructures and maintained the work routine, the ritual of a life entirely spent patching the holes in a dysfunctional city.

"What do you see?"

He remained silent. Tried to catch a glimpse of something from above. He did not want to go down there. The rotten air smelled of decay. His colleague repeated the question. He made a decision and climbed down the ladder into the sewers. They were blocked.

Blocked by the corpses that had accumulated there.

IN WHICH KAHID
ESCAPES UNSCATHED
FROM A MEETING
WITH MACOUTES

Kahid came to and tried to catch his breath. His whole body hurt. His face was mashed up against something cold. He opened his eyes and immediately closed them against the blinding white light. He was in a bathroom. He opened his eyes again and tried to stand: overwhelming pain. He ceased all movement. He didn't know where he was and couldn't understand how he had ended up there.

It had been a long time since that had happened to him.

A long time since he had woken up somewhere else.

He managed to get up. The effort was that of a huge animal dripping sweat, and every muscle shook before he fell back onto the tiled floor. A bull after the final thrust of the sword. He tried to orient himself, to find something familiar in his surroundings. Anonymous and empty, not even a toothbrush. Not even a towel. Dirty and barren. He didn't know this place. There was only the mirror in front of him. His reflection. He'd been beaten. His face was swollen, his lip split. His face was a mess.

He had to get out of there.

He reached the door. Heard a noise and hesitated. Froze with his hand on the doorknob. Two people were talking. He couldn't make out what they were saying. He felt pain shoot through his right leg and he had to sit down on the edge of the tub. Convinced now that he had to wait a little longer before deciding to make introductions. The hand that he drew over his face reminded him that the night had been long.

He cursed Hue. Mr. Tavernak. O'Donnell. The city.

His memories were fragmented and erratic. Another night spent haunting the bars. He was looking for O'Donnell, who was giving no sign of life. O'Donnell, who was supposed to give him information on the bomb that had blown up the front of Steinman's brothel. O'Donnell, who left ambiguous messages on his answering machine. His search always brought him back to the same greasy spoons and whorehouses. He had stopped in at one of the countless Irish pubs sprouting up across the neighbourhood. It had heavy tumblers and counters burnished by generations of polishing and the raising of glasses. It stank of hormones and vomit and lungspitter smoke. Sinister, ulcerated faces. Images of narrow alleys, shimmering brightly under the new light of the meteor. Someone had told him that O'Donnell had gone into hiding.

Clandestine.

He was going to have to clear things up with him.

In the other room, furniture overturned with a crash brought him back to reality.

"Goddamn Golliwog."

A woman's voice reached him from the other side of the bathroom door.

"Fucking kebab-eater."

"Anyway, in less than a month, they won't be here anymore."

"A month? You think?"

"That's what they say… There hasn't been any more for a long time."

"Do you know what they're doing with them?"

"No clue."

"Hell of a time we live in."

"Hell of a century is more like it."

The voices moved farther away and then completely disappeared. Kahid opened the door. The room was small and its door had been left ajar. There was no furniture at all, only footprints on the linoleum. The apartment seemed vaguely familiar. Kahid scurried down the stairs and into the cold December air.

A garbage truck rolled by at the corner of the street. It was the only thing moving. As if the neighbourhood had been vaporized. Early morning. Then two individuals exited an apartment carrying a mattress that they tossed onto the sidewalk near a pile of furniture. They looked up and watched as another individual threw furniture out of a second-floor window. As he passed by them, Kahid couldn't help but notice the strong smell of tear gas emanating from their bodies.

One voice said, "Another apartment empty."

"That makes fourteen tonight."

Kahid recognized the voice as belonging to the woman he'd heard earlier. He stepped up his pace and tried to orient himself. His eyes burned. He sneezed. It had been several years since he'd had the taste of tear gas in his mouth.

GO AHEAD
AND KILL YOURSELF,
HE SAID

Impatient looks and tension. Kicking the door. It would not give way.

"Open up!"

The concierge nervously rattled the keys on their chain and listened at the door. He heard nothing. A huge fist pounded on the door. The concierge took a few steps back. He was too old for this. He trembled as he inserted the key again. Jiggled it in the lock. Tight-lipped. One of the macoutes impatiently shoved him aside and rammed the door open with his shoulder.

They went inside. The tenant had hoisted his leg over the window's guardrail. Ready to jump. The concierge approached him. The macoute's meaty hand stopped him.

"Let him do it."

The macoute smiled.

The Golliwog threw himself out the window. His body smashed onto the sidewalk.

A macoute tossed his lungspitter on the floor.

A second macoute ground it out with his boot.

FOOD ON THE SLY

Nothing was left.

No white noodles.

No potatoes or turnips or vegetables or rice.

The grocery store was empty. Disembowelled. Gutted boxes of cookies. Dented cans. The floor was strewn with bits of glass. A clerk pushed the debris toward the back of the store. A fan turned in one corner. The door was still open. It was cold.

"Everyone going crazy," the merchant grumbled with a strong Russian accent. "Everyone!"

This phrase had been directed at O'Donnell, who had just come in. He ignored the old man. Pushed a tin can with his foot, put his hands into his coat pockets. Pulled his hood back over his head.

"Do you have anything left to sell?" he breathed.

With a weary wave of his arm, the man indicated the state of the store. Aside from a few cans, the shelves were bare. O'Donnell shrugged his shoulders but said nothing. He had no desire to speak. He'd already said too much. He didn't want to draw attention to himself. He had stopped counting how many days it had been since he'd gone out. He was almost out of brainade, but it was the hunger that had driven him outside. He had waited for nightfall. He didn't want to linger too long: Golliwogs like himself were becoming less and less common.

"Who going to pay for all diss?" The grocer went on, ignoring O'Donnell. "Who?"

O'Donnell went over to the shelves and found three cans of sardines that had fallen under the bottom shelf. He toed an almost empty box of cereal and decided to take a dented two-litre can of tomato juice instead.

Not one bottle of brainade was left on the shelves.

"So, papi, did you sell anything today?"

It was a strong voice, devoid of emotion. Authoritative. O'Donnell froze. Peered between the shelves. Someone new was approaching the grocer, who spat out a series of sentences in Russian before the dull sound of a fist punching a face could be heard.

"Shut up, papi, just shut up! You talk too much."

O'Donnell knelt amid the garbage on the floor and silently watched the scene. Another man joined the first. Macoutes, for sure. They scoured the neighbourhood and beat up all the Golliwogs. The second one rummaged through his jacket pocket. The steel of a .357 magnum gleamed under the flickering streetlamps. O'Donnell grimaced.

"So, papi, you alone?"

The grocer couldn't say a word: his face was streaming with blood. His lips and nose. His shoulders, too, shaking with the sobs he was trying to suppress. O'Donnell weighed whether or not he could still escape through the emergency exit.

"Papi?"

No response, just tears.

A shot rang out in the room. O'Donnell smelled the gunpowder. Heard the body crumple to the floor. The two macoutes burst into laughter.

"Damn Golliwog," said the one who hadn't spoken yet. He nudged the body with his foot.

"Call the truck to come pick up the body anyway."

The younger one made the call from his cell phone.

There was a moment of silence. One of the macoutes lit a lungspitter. The second one put away his gun. They walked up and down the aisles. O'Donnell hunkered down. Slipped silently under a shelf and held his breath. He could see two pairs of boots. The smell of a lungspitter. The wail of a siren. The macoutes' boots came within a few metres of O'Donnell's hiding place. The sound of the siren filled the entire room and two orange lights rolled past the store's windows. The sound of a motor. The boots stopped. He saw the butt of a lungspitter fall to the floor.

The footsteps moved off.

The garbage truck backed up slowly and stopped at the store's entrance. The macoutes stood in the doorway for a few seconds before hauling the grocer up by his clothing and throwing the body into the back of the truck. Sighs, suspension and activation of the compactor. O'Donnell distinctly heard bones breaking.

One of the macoutes knocked on the side of the truck, releasing the resonant sound of a full stomach.

"That's enough," said a third voice.

O'Donnell couldn't tell who had spoken but it was probably the driver. The macoutes picked up some gas cans. Put them on the ground. O'Donnell stiffened. A coyote caught in a trap. The vehicle's engine turned over again. The macoutes exchanged a few more words before dousing the grocery store with gas.

O'Donnell had all kinds of faults: he was deceitful, hypocritical and lazy. Disloyal and cowardly. He was a thief. But he had a sixth sense that told him when things were getting serious and the survival instinct was well ingrained in him. The first flames appeared draped in black smoke. O'Donnell decided that this was an opportune time to abandon ship.

He located the emergency exit and slipped into the anonymous night. Behind him burned a yellow inferno, its cinders mingling with the snow. He pulled his hood up over his head. Kept his eyes on the ground. He clung to the walls and walked quickly away. He felt the metal surface of the cans in his pockets. "And once again," he said to himself, "I'll be eating for free."

SKIRMISH

"I didn't kill A★★★."

Kahid wasn't sure if he'd spoken out loud.

An excited crowd. Sweat. Spectators hypnotized by the blood. The din subsided. They heard bones and cartilage crack. They could see nothing from the last row. The ring was miles away. He was hot. Trembling and sweating, his intestines squashed inside his belly.

His head, a festering tumour.

A cancer.

Hue had invited him. He told himself it would change his mind. Kahid had accepted and now regretted his decision. He hated boxing. Detested crowds. Detested Hue. He'd had too much to drink. He knew it. So did Hue. An uncomfortable silence promptly settled in between them. Hue nodded his head as he watched the match. From time to time, he stood up from his seat, then hiked up his pants with a quick twitch of his fingers and sat back down. He flicked the ash from his expensive cigars onto Kahid's shoes.

Since Steinman's agency had become the target of attacks, the pornopros were suspicious of anyone smelling of alcohol or behaving erratically. Hence Kahid slept poorly and alone. A few days earlier, he had woken up because he had vomited on himself as he slept.

He tried again to understand why A★★★ had disappeared. Why he felt full of uncertainty and guilt.

He tried to understand the role that O'Donnell played in all this.

He had resigned himself to the stains on his hands. They seemed to be permanent but no one appeared terribly concerned. Zadourof may have looked at them a little longer than most. He wasn't sure. He wasn't sure about anything anymore. It was into one of those stained hands that Hue placed one of the two immense glasses of brainade he'd brought back to their seats.

"So, you think the little Spanish bastard is going to take it?"

Hue adopted a pleasant, detached manner. Kahid could not stand it.

"No idea," said Kahid without truly paying attention. "Which one did I bet on?"

Hue laughed and punched his shoulder in what was meant to be a friendly gesture. Kahid jumped. Almost spilled the drink he was holding.

"I'm not the one who killed her," he spat.

He had spoken rapidly. Out loud. Hue stared at him before bursting into laughter.

"Of course not," said Hue, laughing. "No one believes it either. The little Spaniard doesn't need help anyway."

· Kahid was confused. Why had he been invited to the match? Hue didn't make a habit of socializing with his journalists. He either had something to tell Kahid or he was trying to get some information out of him.

Kahid took a long drink from his cup. He had not killed A★★★. He was sure of it now. He remembered her silhouette in the room, sitting in the armchair by the window. Naked and white. No, he had not killed her. He didn't have blood on his hands either. The evenings of the past year were all sober and lucid. He was maintaining control of his life.

The crowd suddenly leapt to its feet.

One of the boxers was unconscious. Two men jumped into the ring. Doctors, Hue told him. He saw the pool of blood spreading around the head of the man lying on the mat. A great deal of blood.

Thick and black. Glistening under the spotlights.

"I loved her." Kahid spoke in spite of himself. "I'm really going to miss her."

Hue nodded without paying too much attention.

"Yeah, he's a really good boxer."

Hue sat down and lit a new cigar. He turned to Kahid. Each distrusting the other. Hue smiled before addressing Kahid.

"So…tell me everything and start at the beginning."

Hue's smile was honey-sweet. Kahid leaned away from him. Hue waited and offered him a cigar. Imprinting itself in Kahid's mind was the image of A★★★'s corpse, milky-white, almost phosphorescent. The lure of the void, terrible and inviting.

"There's water, a stream…probably the Canal. There was blood, too."

Kahid faltered. Half surprised by his own words, half comforted to find someone to hear his confession.

"The Canal? And what is there alongside the Canal?"

Hue was intrigued.

"Are you following a lead?"

This time, the cigar ash fell directly on Hue's Italian shoes.

"There are bodies by the Canal. Lots of them."

Kahid was whispering now.

"Lots."

He had loved her dearly. And yet—

Hue dropped back into his seat.

"And what does the ZIPPO have to do with all this?"

He didn't know if he could continue; he didn't know if he had the strength. He turned back toward Hue.

"You wouldn't know where I could find O'Donnell, would you?"

THE ARCHEOLOGY
OF BATTLES PAST

A sky of steel-grey armour. The cold paralyzing everything. An old Polaroid photo darkening with the passage of time. The wind blasting through Villanueva was enough to make you go mad. Villanueva, with its nameless passersby, frozen in the winter weather. And the already-blackened snow, forcing the residents back into their lairs.

An average day. Commonplace.

Since the factories had all disappeared, the Port District had no roots at all. Salt and shit splattered onto the buildings. Garbage cans lined up along the walls of the enclosure. Nothing beautiful, nothing productive. Its labourers had been sent back to the domestic realm with nothing but a kick in the ass. Now they rotted away in the employment centres, captives waiting in endless lines. Before they gave up or were given up for good. Before, with the sky and the occasional vegetable growing on a balcony and children playing in the alleyways. Imperfect symbols of a bygone era.

On an unused section of McCarthy Boulevard, an old sign scrawled in a clumsy hand had been abandoned an eternity ago:

KILL YOUR BOSS

A★★★ had written those words.

Such a long time ago.

Then the factory smoke disappeared, only to be replaced by clouds of tear gas. And riots. Fires and abandonment. Even the macoutes wouldn't set foot inside the Port District. The skin and bones and the filth had no need for protection. The macoutes had taken their posts on the periphery to make sure that the inhabitants could not leave: a zoo with its animals caged. With the jobs gone and the violence and the macoutes rising rigid above the city like prison bars, the residents did not believe it was possible to sink any lower.

And yet—

TIN WHICH KAHID
CONFRONTS O'DONNELL

"Open up!"

The apartment door shook on its hinges.

O'Donnell finally opened it. He was old and grey. He stank.

"How'd you find me?"

Kahid was beside himself.

He pushed O'Donnell inside; he pulled the curtain that hid the only window in the apartment.

Anxious glances outside. It was still night. O'Donnell slumped down on an old sofa that smelled of urine. Kahid remained standing. He was jumpy, electric. It hadn't taken long to find him. Hue had a long reach. Kahid had gone there right after the bout.

"You shouldn't be here."

O'Donnell's voice was tired and heavy. He raised a bottle of brainade to his lips. He was wearing only his boxers.

"Is something wrong?"

O'Donnell sighed. Shrugged his shoulders.

"I wasn't born here, you know…I had to go into hiding, find a new neighbourhood. It's only temporary, I guess…I'll be leaving soon anyway…the super here belongs to the local macoutes. It's only a question of time before they..."

O'Donnell didn't finish his sentence. He stared into his bottle of booze.

"Ever since they took the Golliwogs' right to housing," he began again, "it's highly unlikely that Villanueva..."

Kahid wasn't there to listen to him whine so he cut him short.

"You have to tell me everything."

"What do you want to know?"

"The Canal. A***. All of it," Kahid screamed.

"There's nothing to tell."

"What do you mean 'there's nothing to tell'?"

Kahid was shouting. O'Donnell was not a man who was easily impressed. He thrust his chest out and stared into Kahid's eyes.

"Weren't you with us that night?" Kahid continued in the same tone. "Why are you refusing to tell me? You want money? Is that it?"

"What do you mean, I was 'with you'? You emptied your gun and almost killed me! I should be asking you the questions, not the other way around!" O'Donnell raised his voice. Screamed. "Get the hell out of here!"

Kahid kicked the table. An unlikely collection of objects flew across the little room. The smell of ash and rancid brainade. Pornographic magazines. Something made a heavy sound. A worried look on O'Donnell's face. Kahid tipped over a box with his boot. He recognized his old P38, which he immediately grabbed.

"Hey, it's not what you think," O'Donnell stammered nervously.

"What are you doing with that?"

Anger, rage and spitting.

"You wouldn't understand…they're threatening to deport me, take away my job. They call me at night…it never ends…I'm not the only one! Every migrant in the District is being threatened…and after that night at the Canal…"

Kahid cocked the P38 and put the gun to O'Donnell's forehead.

O'Donnell's face went white.

"What are you doing with that?"

"You're the one who left it by the Canal! That night, I almost walked right by it!"

Kahid pulled the trigger and O'Donnell vomited copiously. A dull click. A sour odour and oesophageal mucus. The gun jammed. Kahid took the P38 by the barrel and violently struck O'Donnell's head with the butt of the gun.

O'Donnell collapsed full length on the floor.

AND THEY BURNED
THE BODIES

The wind picked up. Coming from the exterior. It blew through the streets. Macabre and enveloping. The street-lamps were no longer lit. The meteor was now providing ample illumination. High above an empty alleyway, a shutter creaked on its hinges.

The wind carried the scent of carrion. It came from the banks of the Canal, an odour reminiscent of something they were trying to forget. Mass graves.

They no longer opened their windows.

No one talked about it.

FINAL BATTLES
BEFORE IMPACT

A scrawny gumclacker had gathered a horde of his fellow creatures. He shouted. His voice guttural, his speech interrupted by fits of coughing. His lungs seemed to release something deep and hollow and he grimaced each time he coughed. Had to stop. He immediately began again. His troops nodded in agreement. They frowned. Sometimes raised their fists to the sky.

It was about the ZIPPO.

It was about the purges.

It was about the meteor and the end of the world.

Kahid had found himself in the middle of the crowd without knowing for certain how he'd gotten there. Involved despite himself. He walked with them for several hours. He blended in quite well with the rest of those who'd fallen on hard times. He felt just as badly and was just as drunk. He had the same dry eyes, small and malevolent, and the same wide grin. Something unhealthy.

"You have to go to the source of evil. Find its roots. And no fear in setting it on fire. Close ranks! Shake your fists!"

The thin man had pointed to the Commerce Tower. He held something resembling a Molotov cocktail in his hand.

He was preparing to light it but hesitated. A noise could be heard: tom-toms, trumpets and cries of joy, laughter and whistling. The sounds of a street fair or a carnival coming from the end of the street up ahead.

From either side, people in the two groups pointed their fingers at each other.

Kahid began to salivate as if he were finally seated before a juicy steak after a ten-day fast. It was the Pavlovian response of a journalist reacting to all kinds of stimuli, but the two groups quieted down to share a silence that almost stifled Kahid's joy.

Whereas the gumclacker group was somber and let the black standard flap in the glacial wind blowing over them, the new group was animated and lively. The inscription found on the shirts for sale at the Convention Centre was also painted on some of their signs, evoking notions of social capitalism and revolutionary commerce. Kahid even saw a clown among their ranks and wondered who would come to a demonstration wearing shoes a metre long.

The silence reminded Kahid of the city's growing tensions and made him shudder. It had been a long time since he had been in such an atmosphere. Something tucked into the dusty recesses of his memory came back to him, but just as he did with his recurrent memories of A★★★'s creamy body, he quickly pushed it aside. Only the wind, which caught the black standard and made the large swath of fabric snap over the gumclackers' heads, punctuated the moment.

The music, the shouts and the laughter had ceased.

Everyone seemed to be waiting for a signal to begin breathing again.

Kahid climbed several stairs and took shelter near the big marble columns prominently guarding the Commerce Tower. The overview this position granted told him things did not bode well. A cloud of pigeons soared overhead.

"Death to violence!"

The nasal voice of one of the demonstrators cut short all expectations.

Then someone threw a sign reading ZIPPO FOREVER in the gumclackers' direction. The effort lacked force and the sign bounced off the cold, frozen ground, breaking apart between the two groups. The gumclackers had been wait-ing for just such a signal. Almost in unison, they bent down to pick up rocks or anything else they could find and launched a heavy barrage at the demonstrators. The most experienced among them already had pockets full of round rocks that they dropped on the ground before the macoutes could intervene. The tall, thin man threw the Molotov cocktail he'd been saving for the Commerce Tower. The bottle exploded and the flames spread across the asphalt without doing too much damage.

"Death to violence!" chanted the demonstrators in a sin-gle voice.

"Death to violence!"

A new hail of stones landed painfully on the troupes. The gumclackers advanced and closed the gap separating the two groups. They would give no quarter. Clowns, imps, marionettes, musicians and fire-eaters: none would be spared. The frontline demonstrators, seeing that the gumclackers were moving forward with faces enraged and eyes aglow, sat down and held onto each other as they sang camp songs. Some of the gumclackers, who had armed themselves with clubs or lead pipes, were quite generous with their arguments.

The blows fell coldly on arms and legs and thighs and ribs.

No mercy whatsoever.

Kahid backed up further, ready to flee at any moment. It was no longer what he'd imagined. It all seemed so real, so violent, and when the gumclackers attacked a llama that the demonstrators had brought with them, Kahid regretted being there. They assaulted the animal with kicks and blows from lead pipes and leapt on it like primitive hunters, carving off large strips of skin running with blood and pink flesh that they brandished in their hands like so many trophies. This time, Kahid had a hard time believing what he was seeing. And even though the scene was unfolding right in front of him, just a few steps away, he refused to see it as some kind of sign that a new savagery had been born.

Only hunger.

Hunger and thirst and anger.

And this stinking meteor making everyone nervous as hell.

There were very few demonstrators still conscious when the first sirens sounded, but just before deciding to leave the area himself, Kahid thought he saw the slender silhouette of A★★★ moving quickly away, surrounded by other bearded men. She fled with the gumclackers. He called out her name, just in case, but the silhouette was too far away. He was not sure of what he had seen. No more sure than he was about why such a scene had truly appealed to him once upon a time.

CREMATORY VIOLENCE

Near the ovens, the snow never reached the ground. The heat and the fascist camaraderie and the crematorium's violence. An oily brown rain fell almost everywhere, leaving a sulphurous atmosphere. Winter began to retreat, then hesitated.

The roadways grew slick and the rats left their sewers. They roamed through the streets for all to see, a cold warning of an imminent end. Under the bluish light of the meteor, the dark rain fell. Something noxious hung in the air. Everyone could smell it. No one could figure out what it was. No one talked about it.

The cars moved slowly, trapped in a bottlenecked funeral procession. Trash burning in garbage cans illuminated stoic, vacant faces. The odour of gunpowder and anticipation everywhere. A dead and rotting god, forgotten in the great garbage dumps north of the city, devoured by hundreds of white worms. An absence.

Now and then, a macoute's car or a garbage truck passed slowly. Parting the walls of rain with its headlights. A flashlight shining on the faces of hooded figures running through the rain. A gunshot, dry as the crack of a whip. The drumming rain accompanied the rolling thunder in the grime-smeared sky. The sound of thunder eclipsing the sound of the traffic. Absorbing any silence, any absence, any thought.

The meteor hung in suspension above the city.

With no disciples, no adoration and no fear.

TREMBLING AND TURMOIL

"You think they'll come?"

Luis didn't answer. He had pushed his wheelchair up to the big second-floor window. He was watching the parking lot. The same odour of feces and urine still clung to the Gates of Paradise. It was the middle of the night. Luis and Maervick had been on duty for almost four hours. They were hungry and thirsty.

"It's too late now."

Maervick didn't enjoy the silence so he filled it by talking, letting his words bridge the gaps. Some of the residents had complained to Nurse Chatterton but she said there was nothing to be done about it. Maervick was a neurotic with no hope of redemption. That was the last thing the nurse had told them before she absconded with the bingo fund.

Maervick had been a soldier. Before. He had hunted terrorists at the turn of the twenty-first century. He had been parachuted into the Aboriginal reserves, submachine gun slung over his shoulder and lungspitter in his mouth. He had returned to peacefully pass the days away in this country, days he had divided between his wife and his job selling cars.

He had no one now.

He was rotting away with the others. In the Gates of Paradise, all but forgotten.

"They're not coming. Maybe they've even stopped..."

Luis turned toward Maervick and signalled him to be quiet. The headlights of a garbage truck illuminated the entrance to the parking lot. They had been on the lookout for several weeks now, taking turns with the others. Waiting. Waiting for just such a moment. They had come after all. Luis didn't believe in it any more. Weakened, he dozed, his dreams mingling with his pain. The faint sound of the radio, the sound of alarms. The light from the meteor. The radio transmitting the voices of government officials stating that the displacement of the elderly was only temporary.

Luis had not gone to war but he had been fired after having given the best twenty-five years of his life to his employer. He'd been tossed out like an old coat. He had been part of the class war and considered it to be the worst of all the wars. Since they had thrown Maria's body out the window, bitterness was his only sustenance.

The truck entered the enclosure. Luis' wizened old heart beat faster. His hand, resting on his thigh, began to tremble. He hated that. He saw himself for what he was: ancient and one step away from the grave. One of the antiques, as he called them now.

A goddamn antique.

Maervick loaded Big Bertha. Solemn. Not saying a word.

The piece of artillery had been assembled in the basement. Despite their weakness and hunger, the residents had managed one last joint effort. Dating from the last century, the old lead-spitter was a steel antiquity that creaked and was cold to the touch. It had been set up near the window facing the parking lot. At such an angle that it could not fail to hit its target.

Luis waited for his hand to stop trembling. He picked up the microphone lying on the blanket covering his knees. His voice echoed through all the other pensioners' rooms.

"Comrades, the time has come," he said. "They are here."

The twenty pensioners woke up. Most of them never slept for long anyway. They were crippled by rheumatism and unable to get around without a walker or a wheelchair, but they still knew what they had to do. No one would leave this place: it had been a unanimous decision.

This would not be like the other old folks homes.

They refused to be pushed around.

The first shots from Big Bertha shook the building and rattled its windows. The pensioners held their breath. They knew that they could never hold out against them. They had decided put an end to it. To have the last word. To die with dignity. The first salvoes missed their target. The truck came to a halt with tires screeching.

Silence.

The desired element of surprise had been lost.

"Fire!" Luis shouted. "Fire again!"

Maervick pulled the trigger again. Big Bertha belched out another salvo and the pavement erupted a few metres in front of the truck. None of the shots managed to reach their target. In the time it took to reload Big Bertha and change the angle of fire, the truck had picked up speed and was driving headlong toward the residence. The angle of fire was all wrong now and Big Bertha was rendered useless.

Maervick rose and calmly put a trembling hand on Luis' shoulder. They did not speak. They had failed just as they had felt alive for one last time. In their rooms, the residents faced the intercom's silence and immediately understood. As the rear gate of the truck stopped near the entrance rose on grinding rails, the twenty pensioners listened attentively to the noise of boots marching up the stairs.

All they had to do now was open the front door.

Only a few seconds more before they activated the detonator.

"At least," Luis whispered, "we won't be going alone."

Maervick had the last word. "For Maria."

LAST RUMOURS
BEFORE IMPACT

Since public gatherings had been curtailed, people no longer wanted to turn up at Mr. Tavernak's bar. His clientele knew that sooner or later, everything was going to blow. The regular customers, however, continued to frequent the establishment. Perverse iconoclasts to the end. Risking arrest to come in for a drink, to maintain one final link with the last remnants of humankind.

Even Mr. Tavernak was reluctant to get up in the morning.

His presence was now like a necessary evil – being there was perhaps the only thing he had left to do. That and wait for everything to go up in black smoke once and for all. In the crashing of matter on matter. Astral annihilation.

Mr. Tavernak's bar still stood as the storm raged around it. Despite the macoutes, the ZIPPO and the meteor. Despite the arbitrary arrests. Plans scarcely formed over empty pitchers already announced these aggravations. Swindles and scams that would keep the macoutes guessing for a few hours. Back-alley resistance, held together with chicken wire.

They watched the current and kept their heads above water. Talked about macoutes and hideouts. About the ZIPPO. Talked about the Brown Plague, that goddamn Brown Plague. It had appeared on the lips and the walls of the city. In their nightmares. It had arrived with the first of the garbage trucks.

With the meteor.

It would not be leaving so soon.

Not this time.

SOCIETY IN KAMIKAZE MODE

The gas floated among the rioters, moving slowly through the noisy streets. A peppery mist preceded the gunfire and the flames of incendiary devices. Naked violence had its veil. Looted residences sometimes emerged between the columns of gas. No view of the whole, just fragments of the carnage scattered like crumbs.

Mortal remains did not lie.

Nor did the demolition of things.

The macoutes had regrouped around the commander of operations. Completely overwhelmed, they observed the scene from the top of the local landfill. The speed and violence of the rioters had caught them off guard. They were vulnerable without their arsenal, their method. Disorganized.

They were used to being prepared. To intervening. To manipulating the element of surprise.

The reversal of roles had been a shock and the losses were numerous.

The deported gumclackers had been the first to attack. Several hours earlier, they had captured the garbage dump in the heart of the Pornopro District. First with isolated acts, then with an avalanche. In just a few hours, the revolt had become a concerted, coordinated effort. They may have been easy to repulse at first but the arrival of hordes of disciplined gumclackers had complicated everything. Then came the violence, masked and armed and unrestrained. A grey zone, turned upside down. Confrontation at close range, mingled blood.

The macoutes surrounded the area.

The district was quarantined.

Had they been able, they would have doused the entire district with fuel, let litres of gas flow through the streets and left the residents to worry, burned by the fumes and floundering in the fear of what would come next. Had they been able, they would have struck a giant match and lit the whole place up like a torch, burning it to the ground once and for all. Flambé of gumclacker and pornopro and Golliwog and any other useless, seditious bit of riff-raff. Something kept them from doing it, something inside under all the muscle and fat: a twinge of morality. They were content to watch from a distance, out of range of the bullets and waiting for orders that never came fast enough.

And today, the world crackled and crumbled. Everything returned to the void.

Most of the pornopros had disappeared, victims of the Brown Plague's latest ravages. The rumour drifted unchecked and it trickled into every ear it found. The plague selected its prey. Society bleached clean before the meteor's collision with Earth. The purges silenced the survivors and ash drifted over the city once more.

Guerrilla warfare had begun in the Pornopro District.

It would soon spread throughout the whole city.

Spasms and nausea within the social structure.

And the ever-present macoutes, waiting for orders.

STEINMAN AND THE BOMB

We're born only once and most of the time, the result is horrifying.

Futile.

Steinman repeated this to herself like a mantra. Her knowledge of the world and her experience: she used all of it to alleviate the pain of this inevitability. She could dismember just about anyone without much remorse and she had broken her fake nails more than once when raking someone's face. Today, a piece of herself detached itself from her body. The ultimate, essential disconnect. Blood calling for blood and for an abundance of it.

The macoutes had eliminated most of those in her entourage.

She had only a few Girls left who were still loyal and a huge heart that powerfully pumped out what she needed to move forward and remain standing. She was on her own and knew that she was. She wasn't even surprised to find herself there. She had done it automatically, without thinking. The Ming Restaurant hadn't changed. She had found it like a bitch who always finds her master's hand. Two of her Girls were with her. Loyal soldiers and completely insane, they would not hesitate to take a bullet if the shot were fired.

Steinman knew it. Had always known it. She allowed them this: it was all they had.

That and the terrible yearning for vengeance.

There was no more room for doubt. It was time to do what had to be done – commit the irreparable. Without quite knowing whom to attack, she would act. She would sooner chew off her own arm to free herself than live with one of her hands bound. And her hands had already been bound too long.

"*Si vis pacem, para bellum*," she thought. War was the only path to peace.

The blood of her Girls blanketed her memory. Hypodermic punctures like knife wounds. Until she no longer could tell the difference. Good and evil. Life and death. Her own survival, above all else. In a war of the trenches, you must think only of yourself. Coping with the macoutes, the clients' violence and the Girls' mental health. With drugs and diseases. With the maniacs. She had always lived with this stress and had always known that one day she would have to go on the warpath.

She was at that point.

Today.

The stairway leading down to the Ming Restaurant's basement smelled of piss and decay. A single bulb lit the space. Nothing had changed. Everything was where it had always been, with the same feeling of anticipation. She had bought the restaurant more than twenty years ago and had only been there once since then. The key she slid into the heavy metal door turned easily. She heard it click into place.

The door gave onto a small, dark room. There was a pile of suitcases and she took one and opened it. She took out a flashlight and lit the interior. Everything seemed to be in order. Dry. The sticks of dynamite were there, as they had been for almost twenty years. An almost perfect theft, from the Canal's expansion site. At the time, a much-younger Zadourof had mentioned it, but nothing had been found to incriminate her. The story faded away and now no one remembered the incident at all.

The dynamite had been declared lost.

The file, closed.

One box should suffice. For what, she wasn't sure but she knew that it would do. There were enough explosives in the room to make a good portion of Villanueva disappear. All it would take was a little fire from a cigarette. Taking just one of the suitcases to the Pornopro District dump would be enough to put an end to it all. At least, so that all would be avenged. For the first time. In the call for blood.

She closed the door behind her and passed a sweating palm over her face. At the bottom of the stairs, daylight cut a grey square into the darkness of the stairwell. She heard water running somewhere. The rain was still falling. In just a few weeks, the meteor soaring far above their heads would eliminate them all. If the macoutes didn't have their heads before then.

Steinman had never been afraid of anyone and gave no quarter. She protected herself as best she could. She was the cornerstone of a bastion of luxury. Without her, old and formidable, the turf wars would begin again. The Girls would be afraid again and the macoutes would resume their rights. She had always promised herself that this would not come to pass in her lifetime.

Yet they were returning the bodies of her Girls in the bucket of a bulldozer.

She had a sixth sense for detecting the community's needs. Kind of a gift she had. Just as it was for all those inhabiting the Pornopro District, for Gombo, whom they had so cavalierly assassinated, for Plasticine Girl and for all the women who were now disappearing, the menace was something from the outside. Something furtive.

She climbed back up the stairs, her knuckles white from gripping the handle of her suitcase. The grey light made her squint. Then she saw her two Girls, lying dead on the ground. She stepped over their bodies. They had bled to death, their throats slit. Both of them.

"I knew it was you."

A man's voice. Steinman turned around slowly.

Zadourof was there, motionless under his wet raincoat. One hand held a gun on her.

"The suitcase," he said calmly. "Hand it over."

INTERVENTIONS

"We've been trained for these situations."

The macoute's explanation, backed up by a solid punch. Mr. Tavernak's usual authority had been usurped. The first macoute held a young man down with his cheek pressed against the floor, immobilizing him with his weight. Arms pinned behind his back. A second one kicked him in the ribs. Mr. Tavernak tried to intervene, to react. He was the law in the bar. A third macoute raised a gun.

"Easy now, papi."

Endure the humiliation and force a smile. Guts twisting in every direction.

"Step aside."

He stepped aside. It had been a long time since he had done that. He felt something rise up inside and lodge itself in his fists. The macoute still had the gun in his hand. Nothing was going well in Villanueva anymore. The boots made contact with the young man's ribs, yielding dry cracking sounds. Anticipation. The barman's heart jumped.

He did not understand. He had called a cleaning company because someone had painted graffiti on his establishment, something about a plague, but macoutes had responded to the call. He didn't understand at all.

He simply kept his eyes open.

Until he couldn't anymore.

Then came the memories and his rage.

"Next time," he said to himself. Next time, he would shoot before they even opened the door.

THE CONSPIRACY THEORY

"You still believe in the conspiracy theory?"

Hue had gained weight. Collapsed and idle in his arm-chair, he was an inert mass. He had let his beard grow. Kahid also noticed the stain on his shirt. "This isn't like him," he thought before nodding his head.

Hue sighed. He hardly slept anymore. The summit and the riots and this tension everywhere: it was bringing out his claws and fangs. He had run out of patience, at least as far as Kahid was concerned.

"You are insane," he spat. "Totally over paranoid. You're not paid for that. You're paid to cover the ZIPPO. These are respectable people. Logical decisions. The acts of *giants!*"

Hue leaned heavily on the last word.

This was not the first time they'd had this discussion. Only this time, they were both exhausted. Hue had been unequivocal in his message. Kahid's last three articles would not go to press. He had tried to cut them down and salvage bits and pieces, but he hadn't succeeded. Kahid was furious. Under the meteor, he worked despite it all. Pissing away his time for nothing. Life, balancing on such a fine wire: a very straight wire and so very sharp.

The ZIPPO plunged its roots into an international septic tank that was filled to overflowing. Steinman had been the first to put the bug in his ear. Pointing out certain links between the Convention Centre and the purges, between the macoutes and the dead or deported gumclackers. People in the community were talking about it. He had not often seen her in such a state. So afraid and wary and lacking her usual self-confidence. Steinman had seen quite a few seasons come and go. She also knew that when the wind shifted, it was always she and her Girls who paid the price.

There had been an epidemic. The death of all the dogs. Then Villanueva's gumclackers growing more and more suspicious. More and more aggressive. Not one day passed without a savage attack on the gumclackers and their savage attack on the macoutes. A growing feeling of insecurity striking the gumclackers and then the ZIPPO.

Striking like lightning.

"Just a rumour," Hue scoffed. "No basis for it and no purpose either."

Journalists and those in power were being discreet. Suits came to check the books. Senior officials from the Department, thick as thieves with the ones running the macoutes' central bureau. No one returned Kahid's calls. The meteor was cited as a pretext. The meteor or a lack of time. The weakening of the machine. Like the others, Hue was convinced that something was going wrong. He just didn't want to hear about it, particularly not from Kahid and certainly not now. Not today.

Receptive, almost open at the outset. Hue had convinced himself that Kahid would be diligent in covering the news. The demonstration in front of the Convention Centre, the bomb scares and the explosion at the seniors' residence. Kahid's positions had immediately crystallized. His paranoia, too. To hear him talk, you'd think a purge was being carried out in Villanueva.

You had to read between the lines.

Listen to what was being said in secret.

"There's no conspiracy and no purge," Hue said dryly. "Just men and women making enlightened decisions about our future."

Hue would not let it go.

Kahid dreamed of A★★★ almost every night now, waking up in tears. Crying and clawing at the walls and telling himself that none of it had really happened. His drinking was also increasing. Drunken sleep, devoid of sleep, suffocating in the distorted dream of his reality. The more he drank, the more he rediscovered the world he had once left behind. In the eyes of paranoiac, a dull grey world ploughing furrows in the earth. No salvation, no redemption.

Colourless.

Completely committed.

"So there's no conspiracy against the pornopros and the gumclackers aren't disappearing one after the other.

Immigrants aren't getting thrown out of their homes with nothing but a kick in the ass. The old folks don't feel threatened and no witness has ever seen a macoute or a garbage collector at any of these events."

This time, Kahid tried to drive his point home, once and for all.

"No connection," Hue muttered. "Mere coincidences."

"And there's no connection between these events and holding the ZIPPO Summit either?"

"None. Pure chance. Unfortunately…"

"And I'm the one who's gone crazy?"

"You've been working a lot lately. Of course you're exhausted."

"Screw you."

Hue gave him a nasty smile.

Kahid grimaced and backed away. He was sweating. He left Hue's office without saying a word. The secretary handed him a piece of paper.

A message left at the reception desk a few hours earlier.

"Who's this from?"

"I have no idea."

THE LAST PORNOPRO

The hospital was silent. Kahid hesitated. It had been that way for several days but the nurse on duty tried to reassure him.

"Where are the patients?"

"Dead. We don't get many new ones."

"Is the hospital closed?"

"No. There just aren't any more Golliwogs, pornopros or vagrants coming here to die in our beds."

Her tone had changed and her face had hardened. The empty hospital, cold as a Nazi utopia. A brown-shirt bureaucracy.

"Where do they go to be taken care of?"

"Nowhere."

"What?"

"Go figure," she said, shrugging her shoulders. "But here, most of the residents agree that it's the cause of all this. Something like a pre-selection before the grand finale."

As she said this, she pointed a finger skyward.

Kahid looked at the ceiling.

"It?"

"The Meteor."

But the message he had received indicated the hospital. The paper was crumpled up in the pocket of his parka. He took it out and read it again.

"Room 451?"

The nurse pointed down a hallway. It was still calm and quiet enough to hear the humming of the neon bulbs. An orderly lazily passed a mop over the corridor's waxed parquetry; a drowsing mother held a child in her arms. Flavourless jazz played softly on the little radio hanging from the orderly's cart. That was just about it: no stretchers, no cries, not even the hint of a conversation.

Kahid didn't know what to think. Everything was blending together, taking the place of something else. Losing specificity. He hadn't recognized the handwriting and he suspected that something serious had occurred. He had tried to reach Steinman by phone. No success. Gombo's sister had answered instead. In a few short phrases, she had made him understand. Steinman and two of her Girls had been caught in an ambush.

Steinman was in critical condition.

No one knew who had set the trap.

The Italian and the Witch had disappeared.

Rumour had it that they had both left the city.

"She trusted you, Kahid..."

He had said nothing more before hanging up.

After Gombo, and after A★★★, now it was Steinman's turn.

All that bound him to his prior commitments and his old convictions, all of it was vanishing. Leaving only Kahid behind. His shadow. A package of lungspitters in his pocket. A Thompson novel in the bathroom. A few dollars and the P38 he had taken back from O'Donnell.

The hope of seeing Steinman's body one last time. Her face.

As he pushed open the door to room 451, he understood that it was too late.

Behind the tubes and wires, hooked up to a battery of machines with blinking lights and surrounded by the sound of a respirator, under the sterile dressings, Kahid recognized Steinman's form. A large bandage encircled her neck. The coma they had induced was not the kind you wanted to recover from. Not considering her profession.

Not with the memory she was keeping.

Kahid approached her bed. He gently leaned forward to give her one last kiss on the forehead.

Steinman. For a long time now. With her died an entire era and an age. She was nothing but the merest shadow of what she had once been.

"*Post mortem nihil est.*" Beyond death, there is nothing.

Kahid's voice in the empty room. He would say nothing more.

He stood. Looked at her one more time before making his decision. Then he disconnected the wires that kept her clinging to life. His hand did not tremble. His eyes remained dry.

"It's what she would have done in my place," he told himself.

"It's what she would have done for me."

A FEW DAYS BEFORE IMPACT

Kahid stopped near the window. The dirty yellow neon bulbs in Mr. Tavernak's pub were worthless in the night's new glow. The black snow compacted on the ground. Cold and slushy. His hair fell into his face. He thought of algae, the south and the sparkling light of the sun dappling the coral.

Why not leave?

Run even farther away.

From where he stood, Kahid could see the pub's interior. He took a more careful look before going inside, just to check on who was already there. He wasn't in the mood for laughter or conversation. He wanted only to daydream and wallow in all that would not come to pass. Only to slake the thirst of what was drying up inside him.

He had no more courage left.

The pub was almost empty. Save for a ragged O'Donnell and a silent Mr. Tavernak. Zadourof sat some distance from them, sipping a drink. Kahid could not hear their conversation. O'Donnell knocked awkwardly on the bar with his left arm. Zadourof raised his eyes above his glass but said nothing. Mr. Tavernak remained impassive and refilled O'Donnell's pint. O'Donnell bent his head over the counter. Quietly picked up his glass without opening his eyes.

He drew the back of his hand across his face.

He was crying.

Kahid decided against going in. He had his doubts. About everything and about nothing but particularly about himself. He was no longer willing to take the risk. He lowered one knee to the cold asphalt so that he would be more comfortable. He rubbed his hands together, warming them as best he could. The snow, the cold and the entire night continued to undermine his morale: Kahid sinking and swimming and in survival mode. An observer, despite himself.

Then he saw himself with A*** again, before, in her apartment. There was snow outside; his shoes were soaked. A grimace distorted his face. Then sunlight sparkling through the coral, the south and the heat of a body: he dove far and deep.

He finally made up his mind and pushed open the door. He took his place at the bar.

There was unmelted snow on the floor. Mr. Tavernak was behind the counter, calmly arranging some bottles. He saw Kahid but kept to his task. O'Donnell had already left.

"If I had just one prediction to make," spat Zadourof in his high-pitched voice, "I'd say that you will be in this exact spot when the meteor comes crashing down on us."

Zadourof stayed in the shadows. He smiled as he raised a glass of brainade in Kahid's general direction. A knowing look on his face. Clearly well ahead of Kahid. He took another look around and sighed before approaching Zadourof.

"You look like something the cat dragged in! C'mon, let me buy you a drink…"

"I have to talk to O'Donnell."

Zadourof stared severely at Kahid. Mr. Tavernak served Kahid a pint of brainade.

"The meteor's going to hit in a couple of days. Finally, there'll be an end to it…"

Then turning back to face Kahid, Zadourof said more directly, "It seems that we've been crossing paths a lot these last few days… Hue slipped me a few words. Do you really think you'll be able to get your texts out? Conspiracy theory and other rubbish of that sort. You think they'll let you get away with it, is that it?"

Kahid remembered that fatal night on the banks of the Canal. Suddenly recalled a crucial detail. Someone had called him. Told him to go to the Canal. Zadourof's voice quickly took on all the importance of a droning fan.

"It's the same thing that's been gaining momentum for years and I let it slide. I let it go… Along with A★★★…"

"She'll come back, you'll see."

The wail of approaching sirens startled Kahid. He stood up.

"I have to find her."

Zadourof was still shouting as he left the bar. "You'll always come back to the same place! Didn't you understand anything? The die had already been cast!"

Whatever he added was drowned out by the sound of sirens.

O'DONNELL AND KAHID

Winter thunderstorms are rare. And the air over Villanueva smelled of burning dogs. Because of the meteor, everything had to be reconsidered. A city obscured, its sky streaked by a lightning bolt every fifteen minutes. With its blanket of black snow and yellowed signs from long-ago demonstrations. The city lay drenched in flames in the midst of its distress and riot police clogged the flow of traffic on McCarthy. Surveillance cameras sprouted from the walls. There were no more uniforms, just people with guns. Heavy boots and the slow march of humanity.

The noise of the sirens had stopped several days earlier. Only the sound of the wind and the shouting and the detonations persisted. Only Villanueva slowly decomposing. In the alleyway, the streetlamp crackled and buzzed. Footprints on the ground. Kahid picked up his pace. Plunged one hand deep into his pocket where the old P38 was still nestled, cold and metallic and hard against his fingers.

His step was sure.

This time he would get to the bottom of things. He was determined.

A hundred metres in front of him, a drunk and ailing O'Donnell staggered near a parking metre. He leaned against a wall to avoid falling, releasing strangled sobs and a stream of vomit. O'Donnell hesitated before proceeding. After a moment, he began wandering again. He had no idea where to go.

Kahid slowly trailed after O'Donnell, watching him.

His hand on the burnished butt of the P38.

O'Donnell stopped. Listened. Kahid thought he had been discovered and he tightened his grip on the P38. Tonight. To reconnect with the past. To reconstruct the memory. The headaches and the emptiness and A★★★'s face: he was ready for anything. The meteor's bluish light behind the clouds, a clap of thunder and the desire to strangle him. Kahid would not back away anymore.

A garbage truck stopped on the boulevard, blocking access to the lane. The doors slammed. Two macoutes ran toward O'Donnell. They were armed. O'Donnell dug his hand into his coat pocket. His movements were heavy and difficult but he managed to pull out a little revolver, which he aimed at the macoutes with a trembling hand. No words were exchanged. O'Donnell fired first. He missed his target.

One of the macoutes fired back.

The charge tore off half of O'Donnell's face.

Kahid had just enough time to hide behind a dumpster. He had seen it all. Surviving. No longer going with the flow. The two macoutes collected what was left of O'Donnell. They threw the body into the compactor behind the truck.

Activated the crank arm, initiating the sound of machinery.
The snow and the wind. A flash of lightning.

Kahid started to run.

IN WHICH WE FINALLY LEARN WHAT HAPPENED THAT NIGHT

His entire body itched. His head was resting on shards of glass. Coagulated blood on his fingers. His eyes opened onto a great expanse of sand. A desert.

A feeling of emptiness. Absence.

He sat up with difficulty. He put his fingertips to the back of his head: a mixture of blood, glass and sand matted his hair. He noticed his pack of lungspitters lying slightly crushed on the sand nearby. He grabbed it. There was only one left and he resigned himself to lighting it. He was cold and wet.

How much time had passed?

He didn't know where he was.

The sound of water, the metallic odour in the air finally brought him out of his lethargy. The only desert near Villanueva was the Great Plains. Kahid could not have walked that far. He studied his surroundings. It wasn't sand. It was ash, the kind found near the spill action centres east of the city, alongside the Canal.

It had been such a long time since he had been there.

Beside the Canal.

None of his actions had been without consequence. Even his silences had carried weight. Today, it was all catching up with him. Especially his silences. He understood it better now, as if he were observing his own life from a distance. He saw himself from behind, sitting on the ground near the Canal.

O'Donnell. The garbage collectors. Steinman. And all the rest. All the others.

The garbage trucks backing up and the alarms. He was not alone. They couldn't be far away. Near the Canal. Dumping the ash from the bodies and death. Sometimes the bodies were still clinging to life. No one was concerned about those who remained. The meteor's light was blinding them all.

He had never written anything about the Canal.

He hadn't been back there since A*** had disappeared.

Feelings of guilt enveloped him like his lungspitter's smoke. He thought about A***. Here. A chain of memories. And then one in particular separated itself from the rest.

One evening like any other, not so long ago, in his apartment. Naked and cloaked in cigarette smoke, bottles on the floor. Drunk as usual. The telephone rang.

"Don't answer," he thought. The sound shot through his head like an electrical charge before he stretched his arm out toward the receiver.

"Yeah?"

Crackling on the line. The sound of water flowing. Maybe a river.

He was sitting on his bed.

"Hello?"

Lit another lungspitter.

Then a voice slowly emerged from the other end of the line.

He squinted. Concentrated. He began to hear something.

"Full…of…it's full…"

The voice was lost in the static on the line.

"O'Donnell?"

"The Canal…"

He hung up. Thought for a moment. The Canal. It was O'Donnell. Was he crying? He thought about it again. He didn't know why, but he found the idea of going to the Canal particularly unpleasant.

He made up his mind, got dressed and put on his parka. He put his hand on the doorknob. Hesitated again and turned back. Opened his closet. There was a box sitting on one of the shelves. He opened it and took out his old P38. Put it into his pocket. He left the apartment.

In the stairwell, he sneezed.

Now all the details came flooding back. One by one, torn from his memory.

The Canal was poorly lit. An odour of death. A cold wind, biting. A silhouette came forward into the yellow light

of a single streetlamp like a soloist taking the stage. Everything else was dark. Opaque and dense. The figure brought
a hand to its mouth and the red glow of a lungspitter rose
to its lips in the darkness. An overcoat, hunch-backed. It was
O'Donnell.

He approached. His footsteps in the silence announced
his arrival. O'Donnell shuddered.

"You came?"

His face had been staved in by hunger or fatigue. A grimace ran across its lower half. In an alcoholic fog, Kahid
staggered.

"What do you want?"

"You know about the Canal?"

"What about it?"

"Have you already been here?"

Kahid was distracted. Someone was coming toward
them. The clicking of heels on the pavement, that certain
gait. A★★★ was there, too. Beside the Canal.

Kahid called to her.

The silhouette froze.

"You knew about the Canal?" O'Donnell repeated.

Kahid hesitated. His mouth felt pasty and his tongue felt
as thick as a big bulky sponge.

His mind was elsewhere.

"Write about the deaths! You should have…"

Kahid did not remember having answered. He remembered having interrupted him. His response had been

strictly physical. Open revolt that had become foreign to him. He had wanted to silence her, intimidate her, control the moment.

He didn't want to hear this.

"There's nothing to say. Nothing at all."

"And Niko? And Granite? You have nothing to say? And all our friends from the Argentik?"

Kahid knew it all but he had decided to do his work properly. Follow the official versions. Which contradicted the facts put forth by O'Donnell. On that day, the day A★★★ had left. The day when she had shown him a revolting image of himself: Kahid the collaborationist. On that day, he understood that O'Donnell had a human heart. He also understood that A★★★ was much more than he had thought she was. A fortress.

A conscience.

A constant judgment and a transcendence.

"Presumptions," he had replied. "Rumours."

He had spoken just as Hue had a few hours earlier.

He had said nothing. He had unholstered his gun. Taken out the P38. He had fired into the air over his head until the cylinder was empty. Shooting bright bands of light across the darkness. He just wanted to shut him up. He let the gun fall to the ground. Here, the images became confused again. A★★★ and O'Donnell, or was it only A★★★? His memory suddenly unravelled as it did each time he thought of her. At the Canal. And then he had finally made his escape, leaving the gun behind. He had left them there. Not wanting to hear another thing.

That night, Kahid had decided he would no longer look back.

He had become some fugitive millenarian. Disengaged, absent and cynical.

He had calmly resigned himself to flight. To flight and to silence.

All this passion and outrage. All this anger.

He missed it as much as he missed A★★★'s long legs, as much as he missed her lips and her eyes. He'd swapped his former life for a title, for permanence. For stability.

He was only a shadow of what he had once been and O'Donnell was the first one to have reflected this image back at him. That night.

With A★★★.

He got up and went off in an as-yet unknown direction. The bleeding had stopped but his head throbbed with intense pain. If he'd walked all the way there, it was because something was still working away at his insides. If he'd made it there, it's because he was eating himself up inside. He sank into the desert of ash with a determination he hadn't felt for years.

MACOUTES

"Honey, wake up. Wake up!"

"Unh…"

"I think the macoutes are beating up our neighbour. What should I do?"

"… What?"

"Wait… No… It's okay, they stopped. Go back to sleep."

"…"

FINAL FIREWORKS
BEFORE IMPACT

The Convention Centre's doors were closed. Kahid, in the silent confusion. A sudden end to the carnival. There was neither a crowd nor great demonstrations. Neither Suits nor bodyguards. No more vendors selling cheap souvenirs. On the deserted steps, a chubby security guard twisted a big flashlight in his hands.

It was cold. Kahid scowled fiercely.

The past few nights had been horrible.

Images of the Canal stuck to his skin. In his head. Greasy and foul.

"Where are the others?"

The guard walked slowly toward Kahid.

"Where is the ZIPPO Summit?" he persisted.

"The Summit? Poor you, it's been cancelled."

The guard used the end of his flashlight to point out a piece of paper posted on the Convention Centre's door.

"Cancelled?"

SUMMIT CANCELLED

Small letters on a paper glued to the door, announcing the end of the ZIPPO. Unambiguous. Dissolution. The paper mentioned the reincarnation of the project from a free-trade zone using a different acronym. New parameters and new players.

"In any case, no one really believed in it."

Zadourof was leaning against one of the centre's wide columns. He was rolling a lungspitter between his tobacco-stained fingers.

"What's going on?" Kahid asked.

"The inevitable. The expression of the various faces of our alienation."

Zadourof raised his head after planting the lungspitter between his lips. He lit it. Squinted his eyes.

"And the Summit? And all the decisions? And…"

"Tell me you honestly think this is where decisions were made?"

Zadourof interrupted Kahid, his voice more abrupt, more authoritarian.

"You sincerely believe that the directors would let us in on their negotiations? That they would show us the scope of their power? Of their stupidity? You think they would have been that dumb?"

"But they said…"

"They already said too much."

Zadourof opened his overcoat just enough to show Kahid what he was hiding: sticks of dynamite, little flashing lights and a tangle of wires.

Zadourof smiled sadly. Closed his coat. He sucked more heavily on his lungspitter.

"You went to the Canal?"

The question had been asked with no real expectation. Almost out of spite.

"You know about the Canal, too?" Kahid asked.

Too much information was coming all at once. Kahid was tired, too, and his hands shook. He should have been indignant, he should have rebelled. Shouted. He was missing something, something as vital as a heart or lungs. Since A★★★'s disappearance, he found he had nothing left to say.

"The whole world knew about the Canal. Hue knew. I knew. Everyone knew. One day or the next. Then everyone forgot about it. That's all. Time passed and it just grew stale."

"I never knew. If I had known…"

"If you'd known," Zadourof interrupted again, "and believe me, you knew, you would've done exactly what the others did. You'd have shoved the problem down deep inside, put it in some rotten corner of your conscience. And while the city cleaned itself up and the streets became safe again and you no longer feared for yourself or for your kids, the bodies were piling up. But don't worry, you'll forget just like you've already forgotten."

"Something has to be done…"

Zadourof pointed a finger to the sky, indicating the meteor. It now glowed with a white and incandescent light. Its heat was more palpable, too.

"A few more days, max."

Kahid felt it all like a heavy blow. He sat down on one of the steps leading up to the Convention Centre. Zadourof still stood nearby. He took one last drag of his lungspitter before tossing it on the ground.

"Now get the hell out of here."

"What are you going to do?"

"Get my integrity back."

Kahid stood. Something burned brightly in Zadourof's eyes. Something that made Kahid back away. He had just had enough time to make his escape before he felt the explosion behind him. The jolt lifted him off the ground and threw him several metres through the air. When he came to, the Convention Centre was on fire. A thick black cloud of smoke rose up from a large crater.

THERE MAY STILL BE TIME

"Pour me another!"

The man banged his empty pint on the counter.

"Gimme another one!"

Mr. Tavernak said nothing. Served another drink.

"You know that story, Mr. Tavernak? The one about the prisoners from Villanueva?"

"No."

"So, Mr. Tavernak, there are two prisoners from Villanueva in a cell. And two others, from Riverside, in another cell. They want to escape, see, so one of the guys from Riverside tries to climb the wall of the cell. A really grimy cell. And the other guy from Riverside rushes over to give him a leg up. You understand? To help him get out, see? And the guy manages to escape and that's that. Meanwhile in the other cell, one of the Villanueva guys tries to do the same thing by scaling the wall and you know what, Mr. Tavernak, you know what the other idiot from Villanueva's doing the whole time? Take a guess."

Mr. Tavernak just looked at the man.

"He's hanging onto the guy's legs for dear life. He yanks him back down into the cell. Do you get it, Mr. Tavernak? Do you understand that this idiot, this *jackass*, Mr. Tavernak, he was from Villanueva and he pulls on the other guy as hard as he can so he won't be alone in that cell."

IMPACT

Today.

Today is the day when everything would come to an end. The announcement was everywhere. Had been for a long time.

The black snow melted in the streets. The meteor's heat. The mercury that rose every hour. The light, growing whiter and whiter. The silence, striking and definitive. The tops of the buildings wore fringes of peppery clouds. For some, the struggle and the repression continued until the very last minute.

Kahid appreciated the moment.

He was serene, calm. He had an ample supply of lungspitters and something to write. He had only one regret. That he had given up, let himself be beaten. That he had lowered his fists. Forgotten the constant exercise of his critical sense. He regretted having complied for comfort and having bartered away his convictions. Having ceased to resist.

Things might have been different if...

He was totally convinced. He remembered the waves of populism, intolerance and racism. The rise of the right throughout the world. Discussions about security and the violation of personal freedoms. He remembered the attacks and the wars, the deaths and the blood. Hundreds of conflicts that had filled the mass graves and communal pits. Mass graves in response to the majority's inaction. Trade agreements leaving genocides in their wake.

He took one last look at the sky. The light and the heat were such that he could not stay outside for long. The specialists had warned the population about the combustion phenomena that would precede the impact. Kahid turned the handle. The door swung open to reveal a completely empty pub. Only Mr. Tavernak remained, sipping a drink behind the bar.

It was the first time Kahid had ever seen him do so.

He went and sat down in front of Mr. Tavernak and was served a drink.

"So, are you ready?"

"I think so, yes."

"At peace?"

The silence sealed the moment.

Kahid laid his papers on the counter. Here, when the end was imminent, he felt the need to write. He moistened his lips with the brainade. The heat was just barely tolerable. He was sweating profusely. He gulped down the rest of his brainade. Mr. Tavernak quickly served him another. This time they drank together.

A lungspitter dangling from his mouth, Kahid sought the words to write something important, something beautiful. To mark his departure from this life with panache.

He found only the absurdity of his quest and he pushed his notebook aside.

Zadourof had been right. Perhaps the die had already been cast.

All his memories came flooding back. How over these past few years, he had done nothing but pace back and forth in his cage, how time had rushed by without warning, how the signs, which had been posted everywhere such a long time ago, announced the end of the world and the imminence of destruction. He smacked his forehead and asked himself why he hadn't paid more attention.

Why he hadn't been more sharp-witted and more vigilant.

Today, facing the abyss, a sigh. A reason.

Then Mr. Tavernak directed Kahid's attention to the pub's door, which had just opened.

A silhouette appeared in the doorway. The meteor's light was so strong that it prevented Kahid from seeing who it was and he had to squint to see better. Impact was now only a matter of minutes, even seconds away. The silhouette slowly faded away, swallowed up by the incandescent white.

"Kahid?"

The woman's voice coming from the doorway seemed familiar.

"A★★★?" he ventured. "Is that really you, A★★★?"

...

And then, nothing at all.

Nothing but a great emptiness.

Nothing but a great white flash.

Another chance missed.

ACKNOWLEDGEMENTS

Although there are thousands of thanks to give,
we want to specifically thank David Homel,
Kent Stetson, Fannie Loiselle, Kathryn Gabinet-Kroo
and Michael Callaghan.

They made the English version of *ZIPPO* possible
and deserve a special thank you.